A Quiche

before Dying

*Also by Jill Churchill
in Large Print:*

Bell, Book, and Scandal
The House of Seven Mabels
It Had to Be You
Love for Sale
A Groom With a View
Someone to Watch Over Me
War and Peas

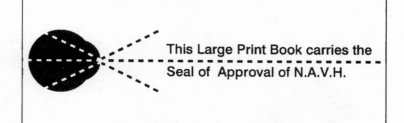

This Large Print Book carries the
Seal of Approval of N.A.V.H.

A Quiche

before Dying

A Jane Jeffry Mystery

Jill Churchill

This work is a novel. Any similarity to actual persons or events is purely coincidental.

Published in 2005 by arrangement with Avon Books, an imprint of HarperCollins Publishers Inc.

Wheeler Large Print Cozy Mystery.

The text of this Large Print edition is unabridged. Other aspects of the book may vary from the original edition.

Set in 16 pt. Plantin by Al Chase.

Printed in the United States on permanent paper.

Library of Congress Cataloging-in-Publication Data

Churchill, Jill, 1943–
    A quiche before dying : a Jane Jeffry mystery / by Jill Churchill.
        p. cm. — (Wheeler Publishing large print cozy mystery)
    ISBN 1-58724-899-9 (lg. print : sc : alk. paper)
    1. Jeffry, Jane (Fictitious character) — Fiction.   2. Women detectives — Illinois — Chicago — Fiction.   3. Creative writing — Study and teaching — Fiction.   4. Chicago (Ill.) — Fiction.   5. Single mothers — Fiction.   6. Suburban life — Fiction.   7. Large type books.   I. Title.   II. Wheeler large print cozy mystery.
    PS3553.H85Q53 2005
    813'.54—dc22   2004025545

Dedicated to
Marjory Hoffbrau and all my friends
at the High 'Brau and Manor
including
Carlos, Evelyn, and the late Jake

As the Founder/CEO of NAVH, the only national health agency solely devoted to those who, although not totally blind, have an eye disease which could lead to serious visual impairment, I am pleased to recognize Thorndike Press* as one of the leading publishers in the large print field.

Founded in 1954 in San Francisco to prepare large print textbooks for partially seeing children, NAVH became the pioneer and standard setting agency in the preparation of large type.

Today, those publishers who meet our standards carry the prestigious "Seal of Approval" indicating high quality large print. We are delighted that Thorndike Press is one of the publishers whose titles meet these standards. We are also pleased to recognize the significant contribution Thorndike Press is making in this important and growing field.

Lorraine H. Marchi, L.H.D.
Founder/CEO
NAVH

* Thorndike Press encompasses the following imprints: Thorndike, Wheeler, Walker and Large Print Press.

— 1 —

"Stop! Murderer!" Jane Jeffry shouted.

The rotund gray tabby cat abandoned his slink through the vegetable garden, drew himself up with flabby dignity, gave one longing glance at the robin Jane had scared away, and stalked off. As he passed a zucchini plant, a sleek orange cat leaped out of the greenery and tackled him. "Oh, no!" Jane cried as they rolled, happily thrashing in mock battle, into a row of frothy carrot foliage. She jumped up from the patio chair and waded into the fray. Willard, a shambling yellow dog, roused from his nap on the patio, came galloping in, barking happily and trampling fledgling crops with his saucer-sized paws. He always got excited when he thought the cats were in trouble with Jane.

"Stop it! All of you!" Jane shouted.

"What is this? Feeding time at the zoo?" her neighbor Shelley said from across the fence.

"To think they were all little and cute once," Jane said, scooping up a cat in each arm. They went as limp as rag dolls, except for the occasional halfhearted swipe at each other. "They should come with warning labels, like cigarettes. Caution: This ball of fluff will destroy your home and garden. Shut up, Willard! I had no idea I needed to put up a ten-foot electrified fence just to protect a few veggies."

"The yard's looking nice," Shelley said.

Jane looked around proudly. Her late husband hadn't approved of gardens. They were, in his view, a nuisance that might draw him into their upkeep. But this spring, the second after his death in a car accident, Jane had gone wild planting. In the rock-hard area where the children's long-abandoned swing sets used to be, she'd planted vegetables. Nothing too difficult this year: radishes, carrots, tomatoes, and three zucchini plants that were threatening to take over the world. There were also some cucumber plants next to the back fence that had run over into the undeveloped land behind her house and were, as far as she knew, producing great crops for the benefit of the field mice. Next year she planned to tackle the mysteries of cauliflowers, peas, and asparagus.

She'd also taken a tentative stab at flower gardening around the edges of the yard.

Again, she'd started with the tried and true: lots of marigolds, some astonishingly ugly coleus, and a lot of vivid red geraniums that made up for the coleus. There were also the good old standbys: alyssum, salvia, and a very puny peony that had put forth only two flowers this year, but might do better next spring.

"You know, we never stayed in one place long enough to have a real garden when I was growing up." Jane said to Shelley. "Every time my mother planted something, the State Department sent my father somewhere else. Want a cup of coffee?"

"I'd love it. Denise is having a hair crisis I'd like to escape from."

"Come on around. I'll bring it out to you." Jane put down the cats, who raced her and each other to the door. They persisted in the greedy but naive belief that she might forget that they'd been fed, and feed them again. They were always disappointed. Jane found the cans of cat food so repulsive that it was all she could do to open them once a day. She ignored their entreaties and took a mug of coffee back to the patio. "What's the crisis?" she asked, handing Shelley the mug.

"Oh, you know . . . slumber party, haircutting at four A.M., tears, hysterics. I wouldn't be fourteen again for anything."

"How bad is it, really?"

"Pretty awful. She has my aggressively straight hair that goes spiky if it's too short." Jane found this hard to believe. She'd never seen so much as a wisp of Shelley's dark cap of hair out of place . . . but she liked her anyway.

"I told her it would grow out," Shelley said. "Worst thing I could have said. It meant I didn't understand. That I didn't care about her at all. That I was a terrible mother. I tell you, if every woman had to spend one week with a teenage girl at the beginning of her marriage, the birth rate would drop to zero."

"I've always felt that way about Cub Scout pack meetings."

Shelley shuddered. "How are you and Katie doing on your own?" Jane's younger son, Todd, had gone on a trip with his paternal grandmother to Disney World, and her older son was on a tour of colleges with his best friend and the friend's father. She and her daughter were by themselves.

Jane sighed. "I was really looking forward to this time, thinking without the boys around, Katie and I could just be girly-girly together. We've never been alone together. But I've hardly seen her. She sleeps late, goes to her job at the pool all afternoon and early evening, then goes out with her friends until the last second before her deadline. All of those activities require that she talk on the phone half the night. I see less of her now than during the school year."

"Count your blessings," Shelley said, but with a smile to show she really didn't mean it.

"I wanted to be closer to my daughter than I was to my mother," Jane went on. "But maybe it's not possible. An innate hormonal disharmony or something."

"I thought you got along well with your mother," Shelley said.

"Oh, I get along with her. Nobody *doesn't* get along with my mother. I think it's a federal law. But —"

"It's just because she's coming to visit," Shelley said. "I get the same way when my mother's coming. It's that funny shift in roles. It's your house, where you're nominally in charge, but your mother is always your mother. Dads make great guests — I guess it's because men of that generation are used to being treated like guests in their own homes. But mothers are always noticing the way you're doing your job. Are your bathrooms clean? Are the kids well behaved? Are your dishes stacked where a good daughter should stack them? After all,

11

we are a measure of how well they did their job. When does your mother get here?"

"Late this afternoon."

"Do you want me to go to the airport with you? It's such a long, boring drive."

"Thanks, Shelley, but we don't go for her. She's got a thing about getting herself around."

"Don't you know how lucky you are? I wish my mom felt that way. When she visits, she sees it as a challenge to find places for me to take her to. It's as if the stewardess whispers to her as she gets off the plane, 'Your daughter is dying to turn her life inside out for you. Do her a favor and think of as many things as you can for her to do.' "

Jane looked at Shelley and grinned. "That's what Katie and Denise think of us, too. We're squashed between generations!"

"Somebody once told me we always like our grandparents because they are our enemies' enemies."

"How true!"

"So what are you and your mother doing while she's here?" Shelley asked.

"Didn't I tell you? We're taking a class. I sent her a clipping about Mike's band performance from that local shopping paper. There was a thing on the opposite side about a free class at the community center

12

in writing your own life history. It meets five nights in a row, then it's done. Missy Harris is the teacher."

"Poor Missy. How'd they rope her into that?" Missy was a local writer of romance novels.

"Money, my dears," a voice said from the side of the house. Missy came around, lugging an armload of books and folders. "Don't you know better than to talk about people outdoors?" Missy was tall, angular, and rather homely. She walked with a long, manly stride and said of herself that she looked like John Cleese in drag. The description wasn't far wrong.

Jane took her feet off a patio chair and helped Missy put down her belongings. Missy collapsed in the vacated chair. "Coffee?" Jane asked.

"No, thanks. These are your assignments for class. Yours and your mother's copies. I notice that you didn't turn anything in, Jane."

Jane explained to Shelley, "We were supposed to write a first chapter to be copied to the rest of the class before the first meeting. We're all supposed to read and critique each other's."

"I think you can learn a lot about your own writing by studying the flaws and virtues in other people's," Missy said. "So why don't I have anything from you, Jane?"

"Missy, I'm not really taking the class; just paying for it so I can go with my mother. What are these two books? Don't tell me somebody already wrote a whole book?"

"Exactly. It's a self-published autobiography of Agnes Pryce."

"Agnes Pryce is in this class!" Jane groaned. Seeing Shelley's puzzled expression, she said, "Shelley, you know who she is — that terrible old woman who's always writing letters to the editor and trying to start petitions — Mrs. General Pryce."

"Oh! Mrs. General. Of course. She's the hateful one who's forever pestering the city council and the school board to impose a full-time eight-o'clock curfew for everybody under twenty-one. Anybody who objects is made to look like a neglectful parent who really *wants* their children out drinking and having sex all night," Shelley said. "She's a first-class bitch."

"She's a career military wife who really gets into the concept of martial law," Jane said to Missy. "And she hates kids."

"That's obvious from her book. Actually, I think she hates everybody — except herself," Missy said. "The whole thing is one long, masturbatory — is that a word? — ac-

14

count of her making everybody she's ever run across do the right thing whether they want to or not. Right according to her, naturally."

"If she's already written a whole autobiography, why is she taking a class in how to do it?" Shelley asked.

"Just to show off," Missy said. "Her nose is out of joint because I was asked to teach this class instead of her. I think she's laying on a campaign to wrest control from me. She's going to be unpleasantly surprised at how difficult that proves to be." Missy grinned with anticipation.

Shelley sat forward. "Is it too late to get into this class?"

"You want to come?" Missy said. "Just bring twenty dollars and I'll give you a form to fill in."

"You want to write an autobiography?" Jane asked. "You're as boring as I am."

"I know I am. But my mother's been after me for years to organize a trunkful of diaries and pictures of our family. She dumped it on me years ago when she sold the house and moved into an apartment. A collective biography would be pretty much the same rules, wouldn't it, Missy?"

"Sure. Come along. Basement. City Hall. Seven-thirty to nine-thirty — unless I bump off Mrs. General by eight. In that case, class would probably get out early."

"What else have we got here?" Jane asked, shuffling through the folders.

"There's something from your mother, of course. Then a nice piece from Grady Wells."

"I'll bet he's not happy to be stuck with Mrs. General." Grady Wells was fortyish, a short, florid-faced, and good-natured bachelor who served in the largely honorary position of mayor of their city. At least it was honorary in pay, which was a hundred dollars a year. For that piddling sum he conducted the city council meetings, attended important civic functions like the opening of the new dry cleaner's, and put up with the troublemakers like Mrs. Pryce. In real life, he was the president of a small company that made playing cards, dice, poker chips, and accessories like bridge score pads. He was a cheerful individual, appropriate to his work.

"He doesn't know yet," Missy said. "I'm on my way down to his office to give him his stack of manuscripts."

"Grady will be fun to have in the group. Who else is there?" Jane asked.

"Ruth Rogers and her sister are coming. You know, the ladies who live at the end of the block with the fantastic gardens? I haven't seen anything from them yet, but Ruth told me they intend to write a joint autobiography. Very interesting concept. They were separated as infants and raised apart. Ruth was in a well-run, compassionate orphanage for a while, then adopted by a nice family. Her sister went to a series of foster homes, most of which were pretty dismal, I believe. They just located each other two years or so ago and want to write a book with sort of alternating chapters about their lives. It could work — if they can write well enough. All too often the people with the most interesting lives are deadly dull writers. And sometimes vice versa. They've turned in a rough outline, but no actual writing, so I didn't copy it to the rest of you."

"I like Ruth," Jane said, "but she's one Mrs. General will smash under her heel with no trouble."

"I don't know about that," Shelley said. "There's a tough core deep in that fluffiness. Don't you remember that incident at the pool six or seven years ago?"

"Oh, yes! Ruth was sitting there with her umbrella and sun hat and books and cute little beach slippers and all."

"I don't remember this. What happened?" Missy asked.

"A kid got in trouble in the deep end of the pool, and before the lifeguards even knew what was happening, Ruth leaped from her vast nest of paraphernalia, flung herself in, and rescued the kid. Really took over. Grady wanted to strike some kind of hero medal for her, but she wouldn't have it."

"What's her sister like?" Shelley asked Missy.

"I don't know. I haven't met her yet."

"Shelley, you know her," Jane said. "Remember the block party last fall? She's the one who made all those fantastic pastries. We all got the recipe for them in Christmas cards."

"Oh, yes. Fiftyish, real frail-looking?"

"Right. Is there anyone else in the class?" Jane asked Missy.

"A couple others, but I'll let them introduce themselves in their writing," she said, patting the stack of folders. "I've got to run. See you tomorrow night."

Shelley had been flipping through Mrs. General's book. She waved good-bye to Missy and said, "What a loathsome woman Mrs. Pryce is! This whole chapter is about how she raised her children. Listen to this: 'I knew that their childish resentment of my firmness, though painful for a loving mother to behold, was temporary and that they would grow up to honor and venerate those high principles I was endeavoring to instill in them from their earliest days.' "

"Ugh!" Jane said. "Imagine having a mother who thought that way. They must despise her, and they probably need a live-in shrink. Maybe we ought to loan our daughters to her for a little while — they might learn to appreciate us."

"Daughters!" Shelley said, leaping up. "I'd forgotten for a minute. I should be home offering platitudes and having them flung back in my face. See you at seven-thirty." She started around the side of the house and stopped in her tracks, looking down. "Jane, I'm sorry to tell you this, but I think your cats have blundered into a chipmunk nest."

"Oh, no!"

— 2 —

Jane rescued one chipmunk and buried another, then she took the cats inside over their yowling protestations. "This is sheer bloodlust and very unbecoming in house cats. We aren't in the jungle, you know," she told them as she dumped them on the kitchen floor. They raced back to the door, pressing their little triangular noses to the crack. She told herself not to be so upset; it was the nature of cats to catch and torture small, cute animals. But then, it was Jane's nature to try to stop them.

She set the pile of folders and the two copies of Mrs. General Pryce's book on the kitchen table and yelled up at her daughter, "Katie, are you up? You've got to be at work at noon!"

"I *know* that, Mother!" Katie screamed down the steps. "I've got tons of time."

Jane refilled her coffee cup and sat down at the kitchen table to start sorting through the class materials. The chapters were in pairs, one each for her and her mother. She set her mother's chapters and Mrs. Pryce's book on the counter and started pawing through her own. Even though she didn't intend to write anything, she wanted to give her full attention to critiquing the others.

Missy had enclosed a sheet of instructions on violent yellow paper that couldn't be missed. It said, "We will discuss these on the last night of class. I suggest that you take notes as you are reading. Remember, writing is a process of tearing off little bits of one's soul and putting them on paper. Writing an autobiography is even more personal. In this class we will *not* make criticisms of the CONTENT of the material. We will only make very kind, constructive comments on the MANNER in which it is presented. You should consider such things as grammar, style (word choice), and organization (overall and sentence structure)."

Jane wondered if Missy had written this warning before or after reading Mrs. Pryce's book. Considering what Jane already knew of the lady and that little bit that Shelley had read, it seemed the logical comment on Pryce's work would be, "Change your life while there's still time." But there might not be time. People said Mrs. Pryce was not only the meanest, but probably the oldest, person around.

Jane was about to read her mother's piece

first, but forced herself to put it aside and skim the others. Reading Cecily's first might upset her. Cecily was, even as Jane was sitting at the table, in the air someplace on her way for a visit. No point in starting the visit without her. Not that Jane wasn't looking forward to seeing her mother, but she wasn't sure what she would find in her mother's manuscript.

One of the manuscripts was presented on light pink paper and typed with script type. The name at the top of the page was Desiree Loftus. Jane smiled. Desiree was one of her favorite neighborhood weirdos. A woman well into her sixties, if not seventies, Desiree had the energy and aggressive outrageousness of a girl of twenty. She dressed in a style that could best be described as "demented flapper/artist," all flowing scarves, spangled headbands, feathers, chunky jewelry, and long cigarette holders. She was still a very pretty woman, with long, elegant hands (usually smudged with artist's oils) and a fall of chestnut hair that looked as if it were still naturally that color, in spite of her age.

Jane was fascinated not only with Desiree's interesting appearance, but also with Desiree's views. She could be counted on to have an offbeat opinion on practically everything. Jane had often run into her at the grocery store. Once, chatting over the asparagus, which should have had platinum tips if the price were to be believed, they discovered that they'd both lived in Rouen, France, for a short time, albeit decades apart. Desiree had apparently taken this as a sign that they were soul sisters, and subsequently bent Jane's ear with her current enthusiasm every time they met. Last week it had been cryogenics; the time before it had been a theory that sunspots were responsible for everything from split ends to the decline in SAT scores. Desiree was so bright and fluent that she made all of her bizarre views seem downright sensible. Jane looked forward to running into her.

Picking up Desiree's first chapter, Jane started reading: "I was born to parents who didn't want a child, so they gave birth to an adult. . . ."

Jane was sorry when the first chapter ended and there wasn't any more to read. The writing was as weird and wonderful as Desiree herself. In a few short pages, she'd made Jane smile twice and almost get teary once. She told of being born to parents who actually liked being compared to Scott and Zelda Fitzgerald. She recounted a visit to an aunt as eccentric as she herself was now. In fact, the aunt could have been a model for the Desiree Jane knew. She hinted at lovers and marriages to come, at famous people yet to be met and savored, at heartbreak and hilarity that would unfold in good time. Desiree was an example of an interesting life coupled with a gift of storytelling. Jane hoped the rest of the autobiography was actually written and she could talk Desiree out of a copy.

"Mom! My swimsuit's got a hole in it!" Katie's banshee screech jerked Jane out of her reverie.

"Katie," Jane said with all the patience she could muster, "don't yell at me as if it's my fault."

"But what am I going to do? I have to be at the pool in half an hour!"

"Well, two solutions come immediately to my mind. One, you could fix it. Two, you could wear another one. You've got a whole drawer full of suits."

"Oh, Mother, they're all gross!"

The words "They weren't gross when I paid for them" were crawling up Jane's throat, trying to make a break for it. "Thread and needles are downstairs in the sewing cabinet," she said mildly instead. She got up to unload the dishwasher — just to drive home the point that she was too busy to volunteer for sewing duty.

Katie flounced off down the stairs to the basement, where Jane had a combination household office/sewing room, and Jane settled in again with her manuscripts. She picked up one belonging to Bob Neufield. She had only a vague recollection of him from the time she had to go to a city council meeting. She'd been there on her husband's behalf when he wanted to widen the driveway and needed zoning approval. Mr. Neufield had attended with plans for a garden shed that would violate the setback regulations. Mr. Neufield, if she was remembering the right person, was in his late fifties perhaps, with a rigid military manner. Very tidy man. Extremely well pressed, short-haired, with a brisk, curt manner.

His manuscript was abrupt and bloodless. He stated his birth data — date, place, parents — as if filling in a resume. The sentences were short, and repetitive with their singsong subject-predicate cadence. There were very few adjectives to liven it up, and no mention of how he felt about anything he was recounting. Poor, boring man! Jane thought, skipping ahead through lists of childhood friends and endless reports of school activities.

Katie came bounding up from the basement wearing the now-repaired swimming suit. "Mom? Aren't you ready? I'm going to be late."

"Ready? All I have to do is pick up my purse and car keys."

Unfortunately, the car keys had hidden themselves, so they spent a frantic five minutes rummaging through the house and hurling accusations at each other before the keys were discovered lurking under a sofa cushion.

Katie's job, as far as the swimming pool management was concerned, was playing with the little ones in the baby pool. In her own view, her primary responsibility was getting a tan. "It's looking good, isn't it, Mom?" she said, propping a slim brown leg on the dashboard.

"It is, indeed," Jane said, executing what her friend Shelley called a "running stop" at the corner. "It's a shame it's not good for you. No! I really meant that conversationally," she said as a cloud of surliness drifted across Katie's face. "It wasn't a mom-nag."

"Jenny's mother is bringing us home, so you don't have to pick me up," Katie said. "When is Nana coming?"

"Sometime this afternoon. She didn't say exactly. You'll plan to stick around with her, won't you? She's coming to see you more than me."

"Of course. I like Nana. She's excellent. Do you think she'll take me shopping? I'm off tomorrow."

"I'm sure she will," Jane said, remembering the last time her mother and daughter had gone shopping and came home with armloads of impractical and unsuitable clothes for Katie. A silk blouse, for God's sake! That was a lifetime investment in dry cleaning, and about the time Jane was starting to feel she had a serious financial stake in the garment, Katie decided green wasn't her color and gave it to Jenny. Of course, Jane's mother had always had a staff to take care of laundry, so she probably had no idea what silk really meant to the average housewife. Jane had to believe that. The alternative explanation was that her mother really meant to make things harder for her.

"Why isn't Grump coming?" Katie asked.

Jane smiled at the fact that Katie still called her grandfather by the name her brother Mike had given him. It wasn't a reflection on Jane's father's personality — he was an extremely affable man — but an infant mispronunciation of "Grampa" that had stuck. "He's in some Arabian country," Jane explained, "and you know how Nana hates to go to those places where they expect women to hide indoors."

"Yuck! I'd hate it too."

Jane glanced at Katie's bare legs. "You sure would. If you went out like that, they'd stone you."

Katie's interest in cultural comparison was fleeting. "There's a great pair of shorts and a matching top at that shop next to the jewelry store. I think we'll start there."

"Here you are, kiddo," Jane said, pulling to a stop in front of the pool entrance.

Jane made a quick detour to the grocery store before heading home. She felt as if she really ought to buy caviar and some of those miniature vegetables that were so trendy. Her mother was used to eating the extraordinary cuisine that the best chefs in the world turned out. But she always claimed to enjoy Jane's ordinary cooking, whether she meant it or not. Accordingly, Jane went through the store on autopilot, got the same things she did every week, and headed for home.

Out of a sense of duty, if not enthusiasm, she did a little straightening up after she put the groceries away, then settled back down with the manuscripts. She finally picked up her mother's — neatly typed, of course — and began to read. Her mother had started out in a third-person fictional mode, telling of a girl named Cecily Burke attending her debutante ball and meeting a handsome man named Michael Grant, who had just started working for the State Department. Jane knew the story, of course, how her mother lost her charm bracelet, and it was returned by messenger the next day with a new charm attached — a silver heart engraved MHG.

Naturally her mother's story started with meeting her father.

The chapter was well written, spritely, and, in technical terms, as well groomed, tactful, and self-controlled as her mother. It ended: "It was as if my life before that night had been a long preparation for meeting Michael. . . ." Nice, Jane thought. A good transition to first person and going back to the beginning in the second chapter to come. And yet, the sentiment left her feeling grouchy, and guilty about feeling grouchy. This was an old, old problem between them. Jane, you're nearly forty, she told herself, you ought to be over it by now.

Maybe Shelley was right. Having mothers visit wasn't easy or natural. That thought took her back to Mrs. General Pryce. Just imagine having a mother like *that* turn up on your doorstep with her suitcases. It was the stuff of which nightmares were made.

Jane sat looking at the pile of manuscripts, thinking guiltily that she ought to be participating in the class if she was going to take it. But she didn't want to write an auto-biography. Her own life, while certainly not ordinary, had no dramatic high points — except a few that were much too personal to share with strangers.

So if she wasn't going to write her own life, that didn't mean she couldn't partici-pate in some way. Just for the fun of it, she decided to invent a person to write about.

She sat thinking for a moment, then pulled a legal pad and pencil from the kitchen "ev-erything" drawer and started writing:

"They say I was born in London to the woman I learned to call Mother, but when I was seventeen I learned that my origins were quite different. The woman who actu-ally gave birth to me — in the rude colonial town of Boston — would not have dared darken the doors of the mansion I grew up calling home."

Jane sat back and reread this, smiling. "Where in the world did that come from?" she asked herself aloud. It was funny — and a little bit scary, how easily that had gone onto the paper. She hadn't really thought it out until she was actually writing it.

An image of a person was forming in her mind. She bent over the paper again.

Priscilla.

— 3 —

Cecily Grant arrived at three in a cab. Jane was writing at the kitchen table, where she could see the driveway, and rushed out to help bring her mother's luggage in, but there was only one medium-sized suitcase. Jane should have realized. Her mother always, of necessity, traveled light. During the whole of her married life, Cecily Grant had never had an actual home, only a long series of residences supplied by the State Department. A few were hovels and glorified tents, most were luxurious houses, a couple had been modest castles.

Jane's father was a cultured, handsome man who had an uncanny gift for languages, being able to pick up the most obscure dialects in a matter of days. Sometimes he used these languages overtly in helping arrange treaties and trade agreements. More often he was sent in to look decorative and mildly perplexed, all the time eavesdropping like mad. Neither his wife nor his children had acquired a smidgen of this language gift, so they made a terrific cover for his more covert activities. In fact, it wasn't until Jane was an adult that she understood what her father's job really was and how important it was.

"Mother! I'm so glad to see you!" Jane said, embracing the older woman. Now that Cecily was actually here, it was true. Cecily carried with her an enveloping air of competence. People in her presence sensed that nothing could go wrong that she couldn't cope with. It was very comforting, even when nothing *was* wrong.

Cecily held her daughter at arm's length, appraisingly. "Jane, you look wonderful. Your hair's longer. It's very flattering!"

"You look terrific, too." Cecily always looked great. She had naturally curly hair that she kept short and fluffy. She never had it set and had let it go gray so that she didn't have to worry about having roots touched up in odd corners of the globe where such amenities might not be available. Her figure was still slim and faintly athletic. She used no makeup but lipstick, and — thanks to an expert plastic surgeon in London whom she visited at regular five-year intervals — she had no unsightly wrinkles or sags in her face or neck. Every time she saw her mother, Jane found herself offering up silent prayers that she would hold up against age as well as Cecily. Unfortunately, Jane's genes didn't

run to curls, nor her budget to cosmetic surgery.

"I wish you'd let me pick you up at the airport," Jane said, taking the one suitcase into
the house.

"Oh, Jane, you know I just get shoved
onto whatever plane has an empty spot. I'd
feel awful if I thought you were camped out
at a dreary old airport waiting for me. How
are the children? Is Todd enjoying his trip
with his other grandmother?" She said it
brightly, but there was the slightest hint of
jealousy. A tiny chink in the perfect armor,
Jane was glad to realize.

"He's having a great time. Mother, you
know his trip was planned before I knew you
were coming this week. I'd have changed it
if I could."

"No, no. I wouldn't want anybody's
schedule altered. And Mike? Are he and his
friend Scott having a wonderful time
looking at colleges?" If Michael Grant had a
gift for languages, Cecily had cornered the
world market on remembering people and
their names. Jane could hardly keep track of
her kids' friends, but her mother remembered all of them.

"Wonderful, but terrifying to me. I don't
want to lose him, but I don't want him to
know that."

"Of course you don't, darling," Cecily said, taking her daughter's hands in her own cool, well-manicured ones. "You're not worried about the cost, are you?"

"Not too much. You know I put all Steve's life insurance money into trusts for the kids. Then I get a third of the Jeffry family pharmacies' profits. I put half of that into the trusts and live on the rest. As long as the kids stay away from the ultraexpensive places like Stanford and Northwestern, I can probably afford it. The only thing I resent is that there isn't enough for any extras."

"You know we'd be happy to help."

"I know, Mom. So would Thelma, but I want to do it myself."

"How *is* 'dear' Thelma?"

"As awful as ever," Jane answered. Cecily laughed.

"Still trying to steal the children," Jane went on. "There are days I'm tempted to let her. Good news, though. Dixie Lee is pregnant, and she's an even more unsuitable daughter-in-law than I am. Thelma's gearing up for a new grandchild to spoil and bribe. Poor Dixie Lee."

"Is Katie home?"

"No, she's working at the pool this afternoon."

"What fun this is going to be, just the three of us girls."

They were still standing in the kitchen doorway, and a pair of cats suddenly shot between their legs. "Where's the cowardly lion?" Cecily asked.

"Oh, he's probably identified you as a terrorist who has come to kidnap him and hold him for an enormous ransom. He's been expecting it for years," Jane said. "Willard? Willard!"

The basement door squeaked open and a wet nose appeared, hesitated for a long, analytical sniff, and was followed slowly by the rest of the dog. He crept cautiously to Cecily, smelled her knees approvingly, and then lovingly leaned against her so hard, she nearly toppled over.

"Willard!" Jane exclaimed, shoving him away. "I'll take your things upstairs, Mom. Help yourself to some coffee if you want. It's decaf. You better start looking over the class work. The first meeting is tonight. This pile is yours," Jane said, patting the stack of manuscripts on the counter.

When Jane came back downstairs, her mother had poured them both coffee and was sitting at the kitchen table, examining the manuscripts. "I'm so glad you agreed to take this class with me. I see the awful Agnes

Pryce is in the class."

"You *know* Mrs. Pryce?"

"I knew her once, to my sorrow. Portugal, I think. Her husband was involved with the embassy for a mercifully short time. They were both terrible people. Mean-spirited and very superior-acting, without any good reason. He was quite the old lech, as I recall."

"Portugal? Was I there?"

"No, it was a year or so after you got married. Your father and I hosted a party once that they came to. Some poor man spilled champagne on her, and you'd have thought it was the outbreak of world war. She chewed him to little shreds. Fortunately, he was an American or there would have been an international incident over it. I don't suppose she's mellowed?"

"Not that you can tell. She's on a perpetual campaign to have all children within a hundred-mile radius of Chicago confined to their homes until they're thirty. Something all the mothers are fighting."

Cecily Grant was skimming through the pages of Mrs. Pryce's book, holding it carefully as if the pages themselves were soiled. "Evil woman. Can you imagine writing down all these stories with pride?"

"I haven't looked at it yet," Jane said,

rummaging in the cabinet for some crackers.

Cecily was silent for a minute while Jane was setting the crackers on a cookie sheet in the oven for a minute to crisp them up. "Here's a story about some poor seamstress in Hawaii," Cecily said with venom. "Pryce says she fired the woman when she wanted to bring her baby to work because the grandmother had died and she had no one to keep the child. Listen to this: 'I told her, of course, that children had no role in the workplace, as all decent Americans knew very well. Though she was very unhappy about it at the time, I'm sure she benefited from the knowledge and later had cause to thank me in her prayers.' The nerve!"

Jane was frantically searching the refrigerator. She'd bought some very good brie as a concession to her mother's visit just the day before, and couldn't find it. Where could a large, white cheese hide in a confined area?

"Here's another one," Cecily was continuing in an outraged tone. "Mrs. Pryce was interned in a prison camp in the Philippines during the war — can you imagine being locked up with the woman for a couple years? She turned in a young woman who had stolen some powdered milk from the stores. One of their own people. The woman was tortured to death for it. Pryce says it was 'unfortunate,' but makes the point that they had to behave in a civilized manner and keep close control of their limited food supply or face the consequences. Grrrr!"

"Mother, are you sure you want to take this class?" Jane said, spying the missing cheese getting squashed under an orange juice carton. Katie must have done that.

Cecily closed the book and shoved it aside. "Of course. I just won't look at this anymore. We can ignore her."

"She doesn't strike me as the ignorable type."

"My dear, I have ignored heads of state when it was prudent," Cecily said with a smile. "What else have we here? Who's this on the pink paper?"

"Are you really going to take this class?" Jane asked Shelley later in the afternoon. She'd run over to Shelley's to borrow some milk. They were sitting at the table in Shelley's always immaculate kitchen. That was one of the great mysteries about Shelley. Her house was always spotless, but Jane had never actually *caught* her cleaning. When did she do it all? Jane often wondered.

"Yes, I think I will. I've dragged down the

box of photo albums and letters, and I've been sorting through it. That's what that stuff on the sofa is," she said, gesturing toward the family room. "What's all that you've got?"

"It's my copy of the class materials. I've already read all of it except Mrs. Pryce's, which I don't intend to read. Mom's working on her copies now, and you can have mine."

"Are you enjoying having your mom here?"

"Sure. She's got a real talent for visiting people. She's really no trouble at all. You know how some people are — my mother-in-law's a perfect example. They'll say, 'I won't put you out a bit, but I don't eat any meat or dairy products or bleached flour, and MSG gives me hives, and do you have the receipt for that blue dress I bought you in 1963?' "

Shelley laughed. "Thelma's not that bad, is she?"

"She would be, if she thought of it. But Mom's not like that at all. She settles right in, does her share of the work without any fuss, and will eat absolutely anything. She does her own laundry without even asking how the machine works or where the soap lives and can unload the dishwasher and get everything back in its proper place. I don't know if she got that way under the pressure of living all over the world or whether it's the other way round. That she was naturally suited to be a gypsy and saw in my father a man who would let her be."

"Do I detect a sour note?"

"Oh, just the usual, I guess. It was a weird childhood, never having a home or friends for more than a year before uprooting all over again."

"But you've got a home of your own now."

"And they'll have to take me out of it on a gurney!" Jane said, getting up from the table.

"Stay a minute and tell me about these chapters. I don't think I can get them all read by this evening."

"Sorry. Can't stay. I've started a fake autobiography I want to type up."

"A fake autobiography?"

"Yes, I'm really having fun. Her name is Priscilla. She was born in 1773 and she has a very mysterious past —"

"Jane! Let me read it!"

"Not now. Not until I mess around with it a little more," Jane said. She was sorry she'd mentioned the project now that she realized Shelley would want to see it. It was still too tentative and fragile for even a best friend's eyes. "I've really got to go. I've got to get dinner ready. Uncle Jim's coming over to see Mom."

"And you —"

"Yeah, but Mom's the main attraction. By the way, I suggest you skip Mrs. General's book. Mom glanced through it, and it nearly made her crazy."

Jim Spelling was a former army officer who'd been friends of the Grants since before Jane was born. Retired from the service now, he'd joined the Chicago police department as a detective. An honorary "uncle" to Jane, he'd kept in touch with her over the years and had been a regular visitor since Jane s husband died a year and a half earlier. Uncle Jim was one of the few people outside the family who knew the truth about where Steve was going when he was killed. Everyone had been told it was a "business trip" when, in truth, he'd left Jane for another woman that very night and was on his way to her when his car skidded on the ice and hit a guardrail. For Jane it was a double loss, but the anger had helped assuage the grief somewhat.

Jim Spelling and Cecily Grant, as always when they got together, kept up an amusing stream of chatter about various adventures when their colorful lives had crossed.

"Remember the time they served sheep's eyes and you had to swallow them whole because you couldn't stand to bite into them?" Cecily said to Jim. "I'll never forget the look on your face."

"And the time in Russia when you went out to inspect a farm in that roly-poly snowsuit and you fell down and couldn't get up and brought three other people down who were trying to help you," Jim countered.

"Mom, I hope you're going to write all these down," Jane said, starting to clear the table.

"Are you writing a book?" Jim asked.

"Jane and I are taking a short class on writing autobiographies," Cecily explained. She glanced at her watch. "And we better get going or we'll be late for the first one."

"I'll stick around here and wait for Katie to come home," Jim said. "Then maybe we can talk some more when you get back. Janie, where are those tools I gave you for Christmas?"

"On the basement steps. Why?"

"I saw you fighting the garage door. Thought I'd look it over while you're gone."

"Uncle Jim, you're a guest. You don't

have to fix things."

"But it's not going all the way up."

"That's all right," Jane said. "I'm thinking about teaching my station wagon to limbo."

"Jim, do you remember General Pryce?" Cecily asked. She was rinsing plates and loading the dishwasher.

"Pryce? Pryce? Oh, yes! The old bastard with the battle-ax wife."

"The battle-ax is in our class," Cecily said.

"Knowing that, you're going? You've got a higher capacity for self-torture than I have. I wouldn't get within ten miles of that woman. She's dangerous."

"Dangerous?" Jane asked.

"Yeah, that kind of wicked person drives people over the brink and makes them do things they shouldn't. Evil *is* contagious, you know."

— 4 —

The class was to meet in the basement of the city hall, which was an overly cute Tudor-style building adjoining the mall. It had been built only three years earlier, and there had been the usual public carping about the expense and style. Its critics said it looked like a Disneyland city hall, needing only a dwarf at the entrance. Its defenders claimed it had dignity and grace. To Jane, it was just a building she visited annually to get Willard his dog tags. The ground floor was a warren of little closet-sized offices for the mayor and the public works people. The basement housed the traffic court, which was, tonight, doing double duty as a classroom. Jane, Shelley, and Cecily made their way down the rather steep steps with a sense of happy anticipation, which was obliterated when they entered the room.

Jane had never actually seen Mrs. General Pryce. Only heard about her distasteful exploits. But she recognized her instantly. Not so much a big woman as an impressively built one, Mrs. Pryce had a pouter pigeon figure — skinny legs, reasonable hips, but an enormous bosom. She was so thoroughly corseted that she looked as if a person could bounce a handball off her — *if* that person had no sense of self-preservation. Pryce had a face like a bulldog; the same prominent, determined jaw and protuberant eyes, the whole unattractive visage surrounded by an elaborate array of tight purple curls. She was, naturally enough, sitting front row center of the makeshift classroom. She must have gotten there a good quarter hour early to assure herself of this position. Poor Missy, Jane thought.

Jane's mother took a deep breath and approached the older woman. "Mrs. Pryce? I'm Cecily Grant. Mrs. Michael Grant. We met in Portugal some years ago. My daughter, Jane Jeffry, is your neighbor."

Mrs. Pryce glanced up. "I don't remember you, young woman," she said bluntly.

Cecily didn't falter. "Possibly not, but I remember you. My husband was posted to the embassy."

"There are always hangers-on around embassies."

Cecily paused. "My thought exactly."

"What is that supposed to mean?"

"Merely that I agree with you," Cecily

said smoothly, and took her departure before Mrs. Pryce could get in another insult. Cecily sat down by Jane and whispered, "I guess I should count myself lucky. I got called 'young woman.'"

"Why didn't you deck the old bitch?" Shelley asked as if genuinely curious.

"Sometimes age is the best revenge," Cecily replied. "She can't possibly last as long as I can." She was speaking just loud enough that Mrs. Pryce *might* have heard her.

Jane wasn't paying much attention, because it had just occurred to her that her fictional person could have a long-lost identical twin. Her mind was racing along with the idea. What if she met a man who'd known the twins. . . .

A tall man came in the classroom. He started toward the front of the room, saw Mrs. Pryce, stopped, and sat at the far end of the second row of chairs. He was lean, with painfully short hair and a stiff bearing. Jane recognized him as Bob Neufield.

He was followed by two middle-aged women. They were obviously sisters, both very feminine, blue-eyed and delicate-featured. One was painfully thin and rather ill looking, and the other prettily plump and quite tan, wearing a flowered dress with far too many ruffles for a woman her age. This sister, the fit one, was Ruth Rogers, the heroine of the swimming pool incident. She nodded at Jane's group and went to speak to Bob Neufield. She exchanged a few pleasant words about some cartons Bob had offered to take someplace. Then she came over to say hello to Jane and Shelley. Her sister, a frail, tired-looking woman, had inadvisedly taken a seat in the front row next to Mrs. Pryce.

"You must come over for tea," Ruth was saying to Cecily Grant after they'd been introduced. "The garden's at its best, and I'd love to show it off. We're just on the corner of Jane's block."

"Oh, I noticed your house when I got here," Cecily said. "Those are alstroemerias around the front porch, aren't they? I've never seen them actually growing — only in florists' shops."

"How nice of you to notice. I've had a terrible time starting them. This year is my third try. They're sunk in pots, of course. They can't winter here —" She broke off, turning to see what was going on in the front row.

Mrs. Pryce was talking loudly to Ruth's sister, Naomi. "Naomi Smith? You're the one with cancer, aren't you?"

Naomi, pale as eggshells, said, "What? No — I don't —"

"Just the same, would you mind sitting someplace else?"

Jane heard Shelley's hiss. "That's unforgivable!" Cecily Grant exclaimed under her breath.

Ruth Rogers, ruffles quivering with outrage, had practically leaped the row of chairs to get to her sister's side. "Mrs. Pryce, my sister has a rare blood disorder. Not that it's any of your business. It isn't contagious, and you owe her — all of us — an apology."

Naomi Smith had picked up her purse and folders and had moved away. "Ruth, please —"

"I don't apologize," Mrs. Pryce pronounced. "Ever."

"Then it's a wonder you've lived as long as you have!" Ruth said. She went to sit where her sister had taken a place. "Do you want to leave?" she asked quietly.

Naomi Smith was shaken, but smiled weakly. "No, Ruth. We can't let that kind of person drive us away from something we want to do."

"Darlings! Are we all ready to be literary?" a voice trilled from the doorway. Desiree Loftus entered with her usual

48

flourish. She was trailing scarves and an exotic scent that Jane thought smelled like a mixture of marijuana and ylang-ylang. "Ruth and Naomi — the biblical sisters!" she said, rushing over to greet them. "No, don't tell me again. I know *that* Ruth and Naomi weren't sisters, but you are. I've been meaning to tell you how delightful the naked ladies looked all over your lawn last fall."

Jane thought Desiree had finally gone over the edge. She looked at Shelley with alarm.

Shelley giggled and whispered, "Naked ladies are those pink lilylike flowers that come up in the late summer. You know, the ones that don't have any foliage."

Jane sighed. "I'm so relieved. I was picturing unclad virgins artfully strewn all over the corner lot and wondering how I could have missed it."

Desiree, courageous as ever, called across the room to Mrs. Pryce. "My dear! Such a bad color for you — blue. You have a red aura, you know."

"Utter nonsense!" Mrs. Pryce exclaimed.

"No, not at all. I'm very tuned in to these things."

"You're drunk! As usual!"

Desiree glared at her for a moment, then

laughed shrilly. "Drunk on the joy of life, perhaps," she replied before turning her attention to the man at the edge of the room. "I don't believe we've met. I'm Desiree Loftus."

"How do you do. I'm Robert Neufield. My friends call me Bob."

"Oh, I do hope I'm going to be among them, Bob." She gave him a dazzling smile and turned to survey the room for other conversational victims. "Jane! Shelley! And who are you? No, don't tell me. You must be a relative of Jane's. It's the eyebrows. They tell everything! People don't pay nearly enough attention to eyebrows these days."

As the introductions were going on, Jane heard Grady Wells's characteristic hearty laughter in the hallway. He came in the room with Missy, who was smiling — until her eye fell on Mrs. Pryce ensconced center front. Grady, chunky and florid-faced, took a seat by Bob Neufield, and Missy went to her desk and started sorting out her notes.

Jane slipped out of her seat and went to have a word with Missy. "I'm cheating. I made up a person," she said, furtively sliding an envelope onto the desk. "Just for fun. Not for the class." She was surprised and embarrassed to realize her heart was pounding at her own audacity. She almost snatched the envelope back.

"What a great idea, Jane. I won't pass it out to the others if you don't want me to."

"Oh, no. Please don't. I'm terrified to even show it to you."

They were interrupted by Mrs. Pryce bellowing at Grady. "I'm surprised you'd have the nerve to show up here."

Grady smiled at her as if she were a grand joke. "I don't know why that would be."

"After the way you've neglected your civic duties."

"Mrs. Pryce," he said patiently, "I'm not here as mayor. Bring your concerns to the council meeting if you must."

"Oh, yes! To your paid toadies!"

"Mrs. Pryce, the council isn't paid anything. And I only get a hundred dollars a year. That's about a nickel an hour for my time." His patience was obviously wearing thin, but he still looked cheerful. Grady always looked cheerful.

"That may be your salary, but I have good reason to think you make a good deal more."

All the amusement had faded from Grady's face. "What are you talking about?"

"Let's not mince words. Embezzlement. That's what I'm talking about."

51

"Embezzlement?" Grady's always pink face had grown alarmingly red.

"Yes. We all pay a hefty amount in taxes, but there never seems to be any money for necessary programs. I believe that large sums of money are missing."

"Mrs. Pryce, I invite you to look over the city's financial statement any time you want. In fact, I insist on it. I'll have our treasurer explain it all to you. But I warn you — if there's any more of this loose talk, I'll have to discuss you with the city's attorney. This is slander and could damage a number of reputations. I won't have it."

Missy cleared her throat loudly. "I believe we had better begin our class."

Jane scuttled back to her place between her mother and Shelley and sat down, shaking her head in disgust.

"Do you think she's gone gaga?" Shelley whispered.

"God! Can you imagine saying a thing like that to Grady?"

Missy glanced at them, silently ordering them to be quiet. "Now, we're all here to learn to write an autobiography —"

"Some of us already know how," Mrs. Pryce said.

Missy ignored her. "I'll be giving you a lot of instructions — rules, if you wish — but I want to make a disclaimer right now. Rules are, as trite as it may be, made to be broken. But the secret to any good writing is in breaking the rules selectively. I believe —"

"Why are you teaching this class?" Mrs. Pryce interrupted.

"Because I want to," Missy snapped back.

"I hardly think you're a suitable teacher. A woman who writes those dirty books."

Missy drew herself up and looked dangerously composed. "Have you ever read one of my books, Mrs. Pryce?"

"I wouldn't demean myself."

"Then you have no right to comment on their content, quality, or morality. I'm sorry to say this, Mrs. Pryce, but if you can't keep quiet until you're called on, I'll have to ask you to drop out of this class."

"I've paid my money and I'll stay as long as I wish. That is my right as a citizen." She turned and looked around smugly, as if daring any of them to dispute this.

"Now see here —" Missy began, then caught herself. She looked down at her notes, took a long breath, and went on with her lecture. "The first thing you must determine is the purpose your autobiography is to serve. There are many reasons for writing one, some therapeutic, some instructional. . . ."

Jane was making notes. *Why is Priscilla writing this autobiography? To explain herself to her descendants? To clear her conscience? To plead her cause in the eyes of the world? Or to prove a point to the woman she believed to be her mother for so many years?*

For a little while she was able to put aside the suffocating tensions in the room. Mrs. Pryce didn't exist in Priscilla's world, nor did any of Mrs. Pryce's victims.

— 5 —

"So how did it go?" Jim Spelling asked Jane, Cecily, and Shelley as they trooped in the door. He was at the kitchen sink washing grease off his hands.

"Not bad —" Jane said, preoccupied.

"Not bad?" her mother and Shelley said in unison. "Jane! Have you gone mad?" Shelley finished.

"What?"

"Earth to Jane. Do I need to get the jumper cables?"

Jane laughed. "I'm sorry. I was thinking about something else. The class was ghastly, at least Mrs. Pryce was. Is Katie home, Uncle Jim?"

"She came and went."

"She's not supposed to go anywhere."

"Just next door to look at somebody's hair. Why anybody'd walk five feet to look at hair is a mystery to me."

Shelley was getting out coffee cups. "It's my daughter's, and it is worth gawking at. She looks like somebody went at her head with a lawn mower."

"I've been thinking about it, and I believe Agnes Pryce is insane," Cecily said, sitting down at the kitchen table. "I remembered her as being overbearing and insensitive, but nothing like that performance tonight. Maybe it's a particularly nasty form of senility."

Shelley joined her at the table, setting cups around. "You might be right. I did some volunteer work at a nursing home for a while. There was a man there, not all that old, but he'd had a stroke. He was belligerent and had the foulest mouth I've ever heard. His family was always visiting and always left in tears. Apparently he'd been a gentle, kind person before. The doctor and nurses kept explaining to them that the stroke had triggered activity in some part of his mind that we all have, but normally repress. I guess his inhibitions had been cut off somehow. Maybe that's what age has done to Mrs. Pryce."

"That woman never did have inhibitions," Jim said, turning off the faucet and looking at the drip with irritation. "This needs work, too."

"Jim, this was far worse than I remembered her," Cecily Grant said. "This poor woman who has some illness sat down next to her, and Pryce behaved like she'd been thrust into the middle of a leper colony. She called another woman a drunk and accused the mayor of embezzling the town treasury. All that before the class even started. That's when she went to work on the teacher for writing pornography."

Katie burst in just then, and there were five minutes of hugging and kissing and shopping plans between granddaughter and grandmother.

"Jane, I ran into whatsisname today," Jim said when the greetings had died down.

"Which whatsisname?"

"VanDyne."

"Oh?" Jane was elaborately casual.

"Yeah, said he was going to give you a call. Hadn't seen you in a while."

"I've been right here."

Jim glanced up from the offending plumbing, surprised at her arch tone. "Yeah — but he hasn't, you know. He's been teaching some law enforcement seminars out in California."

"Who are you talking about?" Cecily Grant asked.

"Mel VanDyne, Mother. I wrote to you about him. The detective I invited to Christmas dinner with us."

"Oh, yes. The fabled Christmas dinner when Todd got sick."

"Todd couldn't help it. I never heard from VanDyne again. I guess he thought somebody always threw up on Christmas around here. Long family tradition. After all, if the president can upchuck at a state dinner, why should Todd be any different?"

"Jane, I'm sorry," her mother said.

"No, don't be. It's nothing," Jane said.

But it was. Mel VanDyne had been her first timid venture back into the world of romance after being widowed, and she'd been humiliated when he never called back after the ill-fated dinner. She'd beat herself up about it for weeks. What had she expected? He was younger than she, extraordinarily good-looking, and sophisticated in the real world. She, on the other hand, was domestic to the eyebrows, wallowing in children, pets, recipes, cleaning products, and PTA committees. What possible interest could a handsome bachelor have in her?

And yet, she'd been instrumental in helping him solve a couple of crimes, and the reason she was able to help was that she understood the suburban life that she was so thoroughly a part of and he didn't. Still, he had probably regarded that as a helpful trait, not a sexy one.

"You aren't going back, are you?" Jim was asking.

It took a second to hoist herself out of her reverie. "You mean to class? Sure. Missy's a terrific teacher."

"Besides, we're committed now," Shelley said. "We've been summoned to dinner at Pryce's tomorrow. A sort of royal command."

"We have?"

"Jane, I'm worried about you," Shelley said. "Don't you remember? Where is your mind? Mrs. Pryce announced that we would all meet for dinner at her house. You even asked if there was anything you could bring."

"I must have been on autopilot. Whenever people talk about getting together, I go into my casserole mode. What did I offer to cook?"

"A quiche," Shelley said.

"What? I don't know how to make quiche. I'd never volunteer that."

"No, it was assigned you. I was assigned a fruit salad — no pineapple. Don't you really remember?"

"I guess it is ringing a faint bell."

"I'll make your quiche, Jane," her mother offered. "I've got a great recipe that uses chicken and asparagus —"

"You don't mean you're all really going to her house, do you?" Jim said. "Why would she invite you, anyway?"

"She just wants to show off her house, I guess. And yes, we have to go. We can't leave the others unprotected," Cecily explained.

"I tried to wriggle out," Shelley put in. "Missy nearly slapped me. She said if she had to go, we all had to."

"Besides, I'm curious to see how she lives," Cecily said. "It'll probably give me stories to dine out on for weeks."

"But why would anyone go? You should have all refused," Jim insisted. He was a lifelong bachelor, and the ways of women never stopped surprising him.

"If we'd had any warning, I imagine we would have," Cecily said. "But, Jim, I've been to dinners where I was expected to eat eels — and act as though I like them. If I can survive that, dinner with Mrs. Pryce ought to be a piece of cake. Now, Katie, let's go sit in the living room and plan our shopping tomorrow. I want to take some notes on your closet."

Shelley told everyone good night and took off. Jane opened the refrigerator door, wondering if she had the necessary ingredients for quiche. She was hard-pressed to remember what went into a quiche. It was just a custard without the sugar, wasn't it? As she was standing and staring stupidly into the white box, Uncle Jim came over and put his arm around her. "Janey, what's wrong? You aren't acting like yourself."

She shut the refrigerator door and hugged him hard. "I'm fine, Uncle Jim. Really fine. And the garage door works beautifully. Thanks for fixing it. I kept hoping something truly terrible would happen to it and I could persuade the insurance company to pay for fixing it."

"I don't think you should be taking this class. It's making you unhappy," he said to the top of her head.

"No, it's really not. I'm not unhappy. I've just got something on my mind."

"Anything I can help with?"

"No, it's nothing bad. In fact, it's kind of exciting and nice. Let's take a couple beers out on the patio."

"So, what's up?" Jim asked when they were settled outside. "Is it VanDyne? I don't think the bastard's right for you, honey."

Jane laughed. "Uncle Jim, Mel VanDyne and I have no relationship at all — not that I'd mind if we did. Just out of curiosity, though, why isn't he right for me?"

"He's too slick."

"And I'm a hayseed?"

"Naw, that's not what I mean. Anyway, I think — well, I think he's younger than you."

"You say that as if it's a dark, dirty secret. He's four years younger than I am. I asked."

"See?"

"That doesn't matter these days, Uncle Jim."

"It should."

"You sweet old reactionary. Well, it's not Mel on my mind anyway. It's something I'm writing for Missy's class. We were supposed to write an autobiography, but I didn't want to. So I invented a person to write about, and I can't keep my mind off her."

Jim looked at her as if she'd lost her mind. "You're sure that's all?"

She took a sip of her beer. "Yes, I think so. . . ."

In the morning Katie and Cecily set off on their shopping expedition. "Operation Desert Shop," Jane called it. They had lists of stores to visit, and had taken a quick inventory of Katie's clothing so that Cecily would know the gaps that needed filling. They planned to start with underwear and finish with shoes, and fit in a lunch somewhere along the line.

Jane glanced at their itinerary. "Mom,

Design Delight isn't in the mall. It's —"

"A block to the west in the little strip of shops with the green roof, isn't it?" Cecily said.

"Yes. How do you know that?"

"We went there once," Cecily explained. "I'll get things for the quiche and be home in time to make it."

Jane saw them off, sorted out a cat tiff, and took a quick tour of the house. For once, there wasn't anything that desperately needed attention. She'd done a thorough cleaning before her mother came, and with the boys gone, the laundry situation was under control. There were hardly enough dirty dishes to justify running the dishwasher, and Katie had not only cleaned her room but, astonishingly, made her bed in honor of her grandmother's visit.

Smiling, Jane turned the kitchen radio to a classical music station and sat down at the table with a legal pad and pencil. "Well, Priscilla, what shall we do today?" she said.

The phone rang at one o'clock. "Yes?" Jane said sharply, irritated at being interrupted. She and Priscilla were in the midst of an adventure, and Jane was dying to see how it came out.

"Jane? This is Mel VanDyne."

Gulp! Nicely — but not *too* nicely — Jane said, "Oh, hello. How are you, Mel?"

"Fine. How are you getting along?"

"Just fine." *God! I'm so boring! Say something fascinating! Quick!*

"Listen, Jane — I've been out of town, and I wondered, that is, would you be free this evening?"

"What did you have in mind?" That was cool, wasn't it? Cool, or just bitchy?

"Dinner, a movie?"

"I'd love t— oh, no. I can't. I'm taking a class. It's not out until nine-thirty."

"Then how about after your class?"

"Where would we go then?" Jane asked, then felt stupid. Just because she was usually home by nine didn't mean the world shut down at that hour.

"I don't know. How about going for drinks? Maybe some dancing?"

Dancing! She hadn't danced for a decade! "How about ice cream and talk, Mel? I want to hear about what you've been doing, and bars are so noisy." She'd probably find out that bars were quiet these days and she'd shown herself up as completely out of touch, but she couldn't face dancing without a couple weeks of practice. Lessons, more likely. The last dance she'd really mastered had been the twist.

"Sounds great. I'll pick you up from your class. Where is it?"

"The city hall. It's not a real class for credit. Just a community thing." What was she explaining that for? *Get a grip on yourself, Jane.*

"Good. I'll get some paperwork caught up at the office and pick you up at nine-thirty, Jane . . . ?"

"Yes?"

"I'm looking forward to seeing you."

"Me, too. 'Bye, Mel." She hung up the phone, hugged herself, and spun around the room. Cats scattered from her path. "I've got a date tonight, Meow. A real, live date with a man who voluntarily asked me out!" She scooped the orange cat up and waltzed into the living room.

Unfortunately, she caught sight of herself as she whirled past a mirror.

"Oh, my God!" she exclaimed, letting Meow escape her grasp. She peered into the glass. "Hair! Clothes! Makeup!" she said to the disheveled image.

— 6 —

Shelley dropped by while Jane was in the midst of a facial. "Oh, you decided to try that stuff? You look like a mummified raccoon."

"But underneath, I'm gorgeous. Wait a minute. It's time to wash it off. Come on upstairs and look at my closet. I need your help."

When Jane emerged from the bathroom, her face scrubbed and shining, Shelley was sitting on the edge of the bed. "What's up?"

"I've got a date tonight."

"A date! Who?"

"Mel VanDyne. And I'm behaving like an idiot. I know it. But I don't know what to wear. Something casual, but not sloppy. Feminine but not girlish. He's picking me up from class, so it has to be something I might normally wear to class."

"Okay. Where are you going?"

"Nowhere much. Ice cream."

"He invited you out for ice cream? What a cheapskate!"

"No. He invited me dancing, but I don't think I remember how to dance. Shelley, it's been more than twenty years since I've had a real date."

"But not since you've been asked. Remember that."

"Oh, sure. The neighborhood sleezeballs who pounce on anybody who looks like they're free. That one who wears the polyester leisure suits is still calling me every month or so. He must have a roster he goes through. And there's the one with the potbelly and load of gold chains who calls everybody 'babe.' You know, he called me a week after Steve died. A *week!* I was so offended that I burst into tears. He took it for encouragement." Jane shuddered at the memory.

"Pink. An apricotish pink," Shelley mused. "I'll be right back." She dashed off and returned a few minutes later with a blouse in a dry cleaning bag. "This is it. Do you have a lace bra?"

"One."

"Good. This fabric is just thin enough that a lace bra will barely show through. Sexy without being blatant. With your white skirt. And you can't carry that hideous saddlebag purse. He'll think you're going on a camp-out."

"You know I operate on the assumption that I might run into Pierce Brosnan any moment, and if he asks me to run away with

67

him, I'll be ready to go."

"Ice cream and running away are miles apart. I have a little white clutch you can use."

They settled on shoes and jewelry and were debating over hose when Katie and Cecily got home. "Hey, Mom, you've got to see what we —" Katie began, then looked around Jane's bedroom. Rejected clothing was strewn everywhere. "Hey, this looks like my room. What's going on?"

"Your mother has a date tonight."

"A date?" A series of expressions crossed her face in rapid succession. She settled on pleased surprise. "Cool, Mom. Who?"

"Detective VanDyne," Jane said.

"Yeah? He's okay. For an old guy."

Jane came over and hugged her daughter. "You just put everything into perspective. Let's see your new stuff."

At quarter of six they dutifully assembled to go to Mrs. General Pryce's. They were going in Shelley's van because it had a flat area in the back where they could set the food without it spilling. Jane had the two quiches she'd made under her mother's direction; Shelley had her fruit salad, and Cecily had voluntarily contributed some cheese and olive puffs and a plate of deviled eggs.

"I saw her make them," Jane said to Shelley in an aggrieved tone when Cecily went back inside for her purse. "I used exactly the same recipe, and when I cook those olive things, the dough runs down and pools. They look like something from one of those obscene bakeries. Hers puff up."

"Don't be cranky, Jane. You do lots of things better than she does," Shelley said.

"Name four. Never mind. I'd hate to watch you struggle to come up with them. I can feel my hair falling."

"Your hair looks great, and if I catch you near a bottle of hair spray, I'll break your wrist."

"Oh, Shelley, I'm acting like an ass and I can't stop myself. Priscilla wouldn't behave like this."

"Priscilla? Who the hell is Priscilla?"

"Never mind. Remind me again why we're doing this."

"Because Missy will kill us if we don't."

Cecily came back to the car. "Mom, are you sure you don't mind my going out tonight after class?" Jane asked.

"Of course I don't. I'm not company, I'm your mother," Cecily said firmly. "Katie and I can talk about you behind your back this way," she added with a smile as Shelley backed the van out.

★ ★ ★

Mrs. Pryce's home was one of the older ones in the neighborhood. It had been built when their suburb was still a distinct town, before Chicago had oozed out and encircled it. There were uninspired flower beds in front and overgrown hedges along the property lines on either side. A not very subtle marking out of her turf, Jane thought. The harsh white paint on the house looked as if it was ready to peel any second. They were met at the door by a maid in uniform. She was an old lady, vaguely Asian, probably Filipino or Thai, and surly-looking. Who wouldn't be, Jane thought, having to work for Mrs. Pryce. "Welcome, misses," she said, relieving them of as many dishes as she could.

Jane walked and was suddenly struck blind in the dark hallway. "The waste-not-want-not school of lighting," Shelley murmured, reaching for Jane's arm.

They stumbled into the living room, where there was a little more light. Shelley's hand on Jane's arm tightened and she gasped. The house was so crammed with artifacts that the eye could hardly figure out what to focus on. Mrs. Pryce had apparently spent the last six or seven decades traveling around the world and picking up everything she could find. Oriental brass figurines fought for shelf space with glazed South American pottery. Spanish shawls covered tables and were themselves covered by Belgian lace and mixes of fake and real Meissen ornaments. Japanese lacquer bowls jostled for space with Chinese cloisonné and cheap plastic pennants. A nest of primitive dolls was stuffed into a big, footed silver bowl that sat on a fragile inlaid wood and mother-of-pearl Burmese table.

The air smelled like a neglected museum — warm, musty, with a faint undertone of mildew and marble polish. There was no air-conditioning, just a few feeble table fans barely turning. Jane supposed the only thing that kept them all from suffocating was the fact that the ceilings were so high in the old house.

She stared for a moment before turning to her mother, who was grinning. "There are bazaar merchants all over the earth who rub their hands together at the thought of her," Cecily murmured.

"I see you're admiring my treasures," Mrs. Pryce said.

For a moment Jane couldn't figure out where the voice was coming from, then she sorted out the visual overload and identified Mrs. Pryce near a window that was covered with layers of curtains. She was sitting on a high-backed chair with some sort of finials at the top — slightly thronelike. Her smug expression made clear that she was genuinely proud of all the junk the rest of them considered so tacky.

"This is all very — interesting," Jane said with a straight face. She heard a noise behind her that sounded like Shelley grinding her teeth.

"Your mother could have a house like this, full of lovely memories, if only she'd planned ahead," Mrs. Pryce said to Jane as if Cecily weren't present.

"You planned this?" Jane asked.

Stunning thought.

"Certainly. All the years that we were collecting, we were having things sent back to storage. Then, when my husband retired, we moved back here and started setting things out. I can't tell you the pleasure it was to meet old memories. It's a shame you haven't done the same," she added, this time speaking directly to Cecily.

"How do you know I haven't?" Cecily asked.

"You're not the type. You girls with the handsome diplomat husbands never appreciate your opportunities. Here! Don't touch that!"

"I wasn't touching anything," Ruth Rogers snapped back.

Jane hadn't even noticed she was there. Ruth and her sister, Naomi Smith, both in patterned dresses, had blended in. They were looking at a crèche made entirely of varnished nuts. As Jane looked around, she discovered that Grady Wells was present as well, nestled helplessly among the knick-knacks on a small tapestry love seat. He had the look of a man who'd just been told his wife was carrying quintuplets.

Jane went to sit next to him. "Are you all right?" she asked.

"Huh? Oh, yes. Amazing, isn't it? I don't think I've ever come across anyone who had absolutely *no* taste on such a grand scale. Did you see the dish of plaster tacos?"

"No, but I saw a wicker Madonna and child and a three-dimensional needlepoint replica of one of Ludwig's Bavarian castles."

He gestured over his shoulder with his thumb. "That room's got a huge hunting tapestry in four hundred and seven shades of brown. It actually has a museum tag that says so. It makes you feel like you've just fallen down a well and broken your leg. Geez! What a place."

They both looked up as Missy came into

the room. She stumbled to a stop, gazing about in horror. Grady's laugh was a happy snort. Missy caught Jane's glance and came over to whisper, "Is this deliberate or has there been a terrible accident with a moving van? How do you move around in all this . . . stuff!"

Mrs. Pryce summoned Missy to pay her respects before Jane could answer. "I'm surprised that everybody's coming to this," Jane said to Grady. "I wouldn't be here except that Shelley told me I had to, and she could be a formidable enemy."

"I was afraid not to come, for fear of what she'd say about me behind my back," Grady replied.

"What about Mr. Neufield? Why would he come?"

"Is he here? Oh, yes. I see. Cowering behind the piano. I don't know. I guess just because he's so law-abiding. If he's told he has to do something, he does it. Army training in following orders, I imagine. Will Desiree show up, do you think?"

"I hope so. I want to see her reaction."

They didn't have to wait long. Desiree Loftus came to a dead stop just inside the doorway. She took a quick inventory of her surroundings and started laughing. "Dear God in Heaven! Has a carnival supply warehouse blown up and all the debris landed here?"

Everyone except Mrs. Pryce laughed. "What? What was that you said?" Pryce demanded.

"My dear old thing," Desiree said, coming forward and shouting. "This is the most divinely gruesome accumulation I've ever seen. How *did* you do it?"

"You don't make sense!" Pryce said. "Divine? Gruesome? Say what you mean or don't say anything. And don't think I'm serving any drinks here. You'll have to get your devil's brew somewhere else. This is a good Christian home."

"Devil's brew?" Grady muttered to Jane as he nudged her gently.

Jane went into a fit of giggles that threatened to become full-blown hysteria.

"Dinner is ready," the elderly maid said from the doorway to the room Grady had described as the bottom of a well. Everyone picked their way through the knickknacks toward that direction, expecting to find the food they'd brought on the table, but it wasn't. Mrs. Pryce's dining table was a long, narrow trestle type that looked as if it had been looted from a dilapidated Spanish castle. There was barely room to set ten place settings, with no space left for serving

75

dishes. They all milled around a bit, not sure if they were to sit and be served or whether they ought to organize a search party to locate the food.

"Take your plates out to the kitchen and serve yourselves," Pryce brayed. She pointed her cane in that direction, nearly stabbing Shelley in the shoulder. Shelley whirled on her and delivered one of her Looks, which normally cowed anyone unfortunate enough to rate one. But Mrs. Pryce was as selectively blind as she was selectively deaf. She appeared not to notice Shelley's glare.

"I'm losing my gift," Shelley said, turning to Jane with a stricken expression.

"No, you're not. She's just that one in a million who's immune," Jane comforted her.

The kitchen looked as if it had been pretty modern half a century before. But since then, nothing had been done except to put so many layers of paint on the cabinets that they looked rounded at the edges. Spiffy white tile counters had turned grayish yellow with age, and the grout was an indescribable color. The ancient linoleum floor had worn down to the bare wood in front of the sink. Filling their own plates turned out to be a difficult undertaking. The maid had set the various bowls and platters out all over the kitchen and the narrow pantry/hallway that led from the kitchen to the dining room. There was much confusion and jostling and backtracking.

"We're like a bunch of lemmings who have lost their compass," Jane said as her mother backed into her.

"I was thinking of trains in India," Cecily replied. "Everybody crowded together in a narrow space, trying to move around and eat at the same time. This is ghastly. I've already put my elbow in somebody's coleslaw."

"Don't spill anything on yourself," Shelley said, squeezing in next to Jane and trying to snake her arm through for a ham and egg roll. "I should have thrown a drop cloth over you to keep you tidy. Go sit down."

"I am sitting down. It just looks like I'm standing," Jane said with a laugh. "It's the press of the crowd that's keeping me at this level."

Jane finally extricated herself and went to the table, balancing a plate. Someone had apparently mistaken her plate for his or her own in the crush and put a glop of something with rice and coconut on hers that she would never have considered even tasting.

Someone must have filled a plate for Mrs. Pryce, probably the maid, because Pryce hadn't been fighting the crowd in the kitchen. She was sitting at the head of the table in regal splendor in a thronelike chair that was the match of the one she'd occupied earlier.

"Where's my tea?" Mrs. Pryce suddenly said to the room at large. Those who were struggling to sit down and finding themselves literally rubbing elbows ignored her. "I guess I just have to do everything myself," she said, struggling to her feet and barging toward the pantry hallway.

"Funny, I had the impression she did *nothing* herself," Missy said.

"Is there salt on the table?" Desiree asked. There was a general shifting as everyone looked for it. "Oh, there. Bob, next to you." Everybody had to shift their elbows around to pass a china salt shaker in the shape of a thatched cottage.

"Sorry, Grady," Missy said as she jostled his arm, causing him to drop his spoon.

"What *is* this green stuff?" somebody asked.

Ruth kept looking back over her shoulder at the multitudinously brown tapestry as if it might suddenly fling itself over her head and smother her. Every time she craned around, she jostled her sister, Naomi, who was picking fretfully at her food.

"Is this part of you or me?" Cecily asked Shelley, slowly adjusting her legs under the table.

"Oh, I didn't get anything to drink either," Jane said, getting back up. "Mom? Shelley? You want anything?"

"I'll get myself some coffee," Shelley said, joining her. The crowd in the hall had thinned out, and there was no sign of Mrs. Pryce. Jane noticed that there was another door to the kitchen, presumably leading to the gloomy front hall. Mrs. Pryce must have gone that way. The maid was sitting on a high stool by the sink, staring out the window and absently picking at a hangnail.

Jane and Shelley got their drinks and returned to find most of the others crawling around on the floor, trying to help Grady find his contact lens. Mrs. Pryce found it by stepping on it as she came through from the living room. Instead of apologizing to Grady, she gave a general lecture on the wickedness of modern things, pointing out that spectacles were good enough for her generation.

"Okay, that's all I can stand," Grady said, huffing a little as he got up from the floor.

"Could somebody drive me home to get my glasses?"

There was a deafening chorus of volunteers.

"I've got to pick up something for class anyway," Missy outshouted the rest. "I'll take you, Grady. There won't be time to get back. We'll see the rest of you later," she said, all but skipping in her haste to escape.

Jane watched them leave, sadly. She glanced at her watch. They'd only been there half an hour, and it already seemed like days and days. If it weren't for her obligation to her mother — and to Priscilla — she'd have run sobbing after Grady and Missy, begging to go with them.

— 7 —

"I think a teacher ought to be like the captain of a ship — the last one off in case of disaster." Jane said darkly to Missy as they came into the classroom.

Missy laughed. "You're all grown-ups, and perfectly able to fend for yourselves. And you *did* survive, or you wouldn't be here to bitch at me now."

Jane slipped another envelope onto the desk. "A little more of Priscilla," she said in a low tone.

"Oh, good! Jane, I want to talk to you about this. Can I come by in the morning?"

"Sure."

The rest of the class was trailing in, giving Missy and Grady dirty looks. Grady looked guilty. Missy didn't. Mrs. Pryce was last. She again took her place center front. Nobody would have dared to take her place.

"I still smell like that house," Shelley muttered.

Missy started her lecture. "Tonight I want to start class by talking about some basic rules of good writing that apply no matter what the subject matter, whether fiction or nonfiction —"

Mrs. Pryce coughed several times.

Missy waited politely, then went on, "First, I have a handout here that lists some good basic grammar books and style sheets that you might want to get. You should have one of these handy as you continue your writing. Grady, will you pass these out for me?"

He bounced up, took the sheets, and started distributing them. As he reached Mrs. Pryce, she grabbed hers and said, "Get me a drink of water."

"In a minute," Grady said, leaning across her to give a sheet to Ruth Rogers on her other side.

Mrs. Pryce slapped his arm away. "Now!"

Grady shrugged and went out into the hall. Mrs. Pryce craned her neck around and glared at the rest of them. "What are you all gawking at? You're all fools!"

"Mrs. Pryce, I'm going to have to ask you to leave if there's one more outburst," Missy said firmly.

Pryce either didn't hear her or pretended not to. "Where has that idiot man gone?" she said. "Just go back to your business. All of you. I'll have my husband see to things if I have to."

Jane felt a shiver of apprehension. General Pryce, if she remembered correctly, had been dead for some years.

Grady came in with a paper cup of water. As he handed it to Mrs. Pryce, she had a coughing spasm. She gulped down the water, choked slightly, and said, "Why are you turning those lights up? You're doing this to harass me. Well, you'll just all blind yourselves in the bargain, and it'll serve you right. You're all against me. Don't think I don't know it —" Her voice was rising, sounding dry and hoarse. Naomi, looking paler than usual and obviously alarmed, inched her chair a fraction closer to Jane and her mother. Mrs. Pryce thrashed her cane around, knocking it against a few chairs before she settled it firmly on the floor and started to rise. But she fell back in her chair heavily.

"You!" she said, suddenly focusing on Bob Neufield. "You got just what you deserved, and don't try to tell me otherwise. You depraved pretty boys don't deserve to have the opportunity to serve a fine country like this —"

Bob Neufield drew himself up and looked as if he'd been stabbed in the heart.

"Mrs. Pryce, you must be quiet!" Missy said, looking around frantically. "What's

83

the matter with you?"

"I'll get you some more water. Just settle down." Grady spoke to her as if she were a badly behaved child.

"You'll blind yourselves. It'll serve you right," Mrs. Pryce said. Her glare had turned to a squint and she was shivering uncontrollably.

Ruth Rogers had risen from her chair; she put one hand on Mrs. Pryce's forehead and grabbed her wrist with the other. Mrs. Pryce struggled. "Take your hands off me! How dare you touch me, you disgusting woman!"

Ruth hung on, looking at Missy. "She's feverish and her pulse is very fast."

"I'll call an ambulance," Missy said, coming around the desk and racing from the room.

Jane looked at her mother. "Is there anything we should do?"

"Let's clear a path for the medics."

Mrs. Pryce was still raving and trying to get away from Ruth, who was keeping her firmly in her chair. Ruth's frail sister, Naomi, was helping to hang on to the elderly woman, who was showing surprising strength. Jane, Shelley, and Cecily started pushing the chairs to the side of the room, making a wide aisle. Desiree Loftus, looking terrified, got up and started helping them.

Bob Neufield was standing back, looking like a military guard who was under orders not to react.

They could already hear the sirens. "Here, let's get out of the way," Grady said, and with Bob Neufield's help, started pushing everybody except Ruth and Naomi toward the door. The women started snatching up their belongings and going into the hallway.

Jane was nearly run over by three ambulance attendants as she left. She slipped past them and leaned against the hallway wall. "I need some fresh air," she said, feeling woozy.

Cecily grabbed her arm and steered her up the stairway and toward the exit. Just as they reached the foyer and front double door of the city hall, one of the doors was yanked open, nearly spilling them outside.

"Jane! Are you all right?" Mel VanDyne said, steadying her.

She looked up. "Just a tad faint. What are you doing here?"

"I was in the station doing some work when the call came in about a woman down in the basement of the city hall. I was afraid — well, I'm glad you're okay. What happened?"

"An old lady in our class had a stroke or a

fit or something. It was horrible." She took a deep breath and looked at him. "It's nice to see you again," she added, aware that it wasn't a particularly appropriate thing to say. Still, he looked even better than she'd remembered him, and he looked especially good when he was showing concern for her. He was a remarkably handsome man, even more so than she'd remembered. Why was it that men tended to improve with age and women tended to unravel? Jane wondered.

Cecily cleared her throat pointedly.

"Oh, sorry. Mother, this is Mel VanDyne. Mel, my mother, Cecily Grant."

"Now I see where you get your looks," Mel said, grinning. It was a hokey, clichéd thing to say, but he carried it off. "I'm glad to meet you, Mrs. Grant."

"Hadn't you better go downstairs?" Jane said.

"No, I'm just a spectator. Nothing suspicious about this, is there?"

"Nothing at all," Cecily said. "Just a very mean elderly lady going to meet her maker — and probably tell him just what he's done wrong with the world."

They perched in a row on the edge of a flower box by the doors. The red lights of the ambulance were streaking blindingly around the parking lot, making all of them

86

and the building turn red every few seconds. Another police car pulled up, and the officers nodded to VanDyne as they went into the building. A moment later, Ruth and Naomi came out the door, with Shelley just behind. Naomi had her hand out as if longing to stabilize herself against her sturdy, competent sister.

"How is she?" Jane asked.

"Dead," Shelley said bluntly. "At least she went out completely in character. Oh, it's Detective VanDyne, isn't it? Nice to see you again."

"How are you, Mrs. Nowack? And what do you mean about going out in character?"

"She was a dreadful, nasty woman. Made my mother-in-law look like Mother Teresa. She had some kind of seizure and was saying terrible things about everybody. What do we do now?"

The door had opened again as she was speaking. "You could get out of the way," Grady said. He was propping the double doors open. Jane expected the ambulance attendants to be just behind him, but Missy, Bob Neufield, and Desiree Loftus came out next. Neufield's face was white and set in a grimace, and Desiree looked suddenly old and vulnerable. She had her hand on his arm lightly.

"Gather around," Missy said in her best schoolteacher manner. "Are we all here? Yes, I believe so. In spite of this tragic and terribly upsetting occurrence, I believe the class should go on. We won't, of course, reconvene tonight, but I suggest we meet tomorrow night at the usual time and go an hour extra. I have a lot of material to cover, and you've all paid good money for it. Is that satisfactory? Everyone?"

There was a faint chorus of agreement.

"Your teacher's a sensible woman," Mel murmured to Jane.

"Very well," Missy said. "I suggest we all go home and try to put this out of our minds as best we can. It's not acceptable to speak ill of the dead, but Mrs. Pryce was not a valuable addition to the class, and I genuinely look forward to seeing the rest of you tomorrow." She smiled at Jane. "See? I don't believe in *anybody* going down with the ship."

They were all drifting away from the front doors when Jane suddenly said, "Mrs. Pryce's maid! She ordered the poor old thing to pick her up after class. Somebody should tell her."

Missy sighed. "I guess it's my responsibility. I'll run by there."

"Do you want Jane and me to go with you?" Mel said.

"Yes, that would be nice — who *are* you?"

Jane made the introductions.

"A detective?" Missy said, alarmed.

"Off duty. Jane and I had a date after class."

"Well, well, well," Missy said, smiling at Jane like a fond auntie. "How nice. I don't mean to ruin your evening, but I would appreciate it if you'd run by there with me for a minute. The maid will probably be pleased to know that her bondage is over, but who knows? I wouldn't know what to do with her if she went to pieces on me."

As they were getting into Mel's car, the ambulance attendants were maneuvering a gurney out through the doors. The figure on it was completely covered. Jane knew she should feel sadness at Mrs. Pryce's death, but could only be sad about her life — her wasted, empty, mean-spirited life, filled only with souvenirs. Jane suddenly realized that in all the trash and treasures, there hadn't been a single picture of a person.

They rang the bell three times. Finally the maid opened the door. Although it was nearly dark, she was shading her eyes and squinting. "Yes? Who are you? Misses, she's out."

"I'm the teacher. Mrs. Jeffry and I were

here a while ago at dinner," Missy said. "May we come in?"

"Yes. But misses not here." She fished a handkerchief from her pocket and seemed slightly unbalanced by the action. She steadied herself against the doorframe for a moment, then stood aside.

They followed her into the front hall. "I'm afraid we have bad news," Missy said. "Mrs. Pryce became ill during class —"

"Yes, yes. I pick her up."

"No, you don't have to pick her up. She's been taken to the hospital —"

"Keys. Car keys. Don't know where — the lawn. Yes. Water the lawn — storm coming," she said, then lapsed into babbling in a foreign language.

Mel was looking a question at Missy and Jane. "Is she crazy?" he seemed to be asking.

"— and then we go to market," the maid said. She staggered, and Jane grabbed her to keep her from falling.

"Mel, there's something wrong. This is how Mrs. Pryce was acting — sensitive to light, raving, off balance."

The woman was leaning against the doorframe, clutching at her chest.

"Where's the phone?" Mel demanded.

Missy tried to calm the maid down while

Mel and Jane searched for a phone. W
he found it, he dialed quickly, identiﬁ
himself, and gave Mrs. Pryce's address.
"Send an ambulance and seal off the city
hall. I think it may be a crime scene."

He hung up and looked at Jane, who was
helping Missy get the maid to sit down on a
settee in the front hall. "You sure are a fun
date," he said wryly.

— 8 —

Missy came by at ten the next morning. Jane had been up since eight but still felt blurry. It had been a late night.

"Can you stand company?" Missy said. She was looking a little haggard, too.

"Sure. Come in. Want some iced tea?"

"Only if you throw it in my face to wake me up."

"Were you up late, too?"

"There were policemen questioning me until nearly two, then I couldn't get to sleep. Gee, it's quiet. Where is everybody else?"

"Katie's still in bed, and my mother's gone to visit an old friend in Evanston. I couldn't sleep last night either. Then when I finally dropped off, Mel called around four to let me know that the maid — her name's Maria Espinoza, by the way — is probably going to recover. They pumped her stomach right away on the assumption that it might have been something they both ate."

"And what did they find?"

"I don't know. Mel says the pathology

people say the symptoms could point to any number of poisons. But they won't know until they've done an autopsy on Mrs. Pryce and analyzed Maria's stomach contents. Ugh! Imagine doing that for a living."

"So that's why they kept asking me about the dinner."

"I guess so. The man who interviewed me wanted to know who'd brought what."

"I assume they're considering it a deliberate poisoning?" Missy asked.

"I don't know what else it could be. I mean, if a poison had accidentally been in any of the dishes, more than two people would have gotten sick. We were all pretty polite about trying a little of everything. And if it had been some weird allergic reaction, it probably would have affected only one person. But it's crazy anyway."

"What do you mean?"

"Just that she was a first-class bitch, but so are lots of people, and they don't get killed. If this was poisoning and it was deliberate, it means one of the people in the class might have done it, and that's unbelievable."

"Unlikely, I'll grant," Missy said. "I think I will take you up on that tea offer, if you don't mind."

"Okay. Let's take them outside while it's

still nice. It's supposed to be in the nineties later today."

It was already warm, but still just barely pleasant outdoors. There had been a little rain overnight, and the garden looked refreshed. Willard came out with them for a little romp in the vegetables before he got on with the doggy business of barking at birds.

"It's more than just unlikely that it was someone in class," Jane continued as they settled themselves under the patio umbrella. She yelled at Willard, who reluctantly came back and flopped down under her chair. "Killing somebody must be a huge thing in a person's life. If you were given to murdering people just because they were annoying as hell, you'd give in to the urge early in life, wouldn't you?"

"I'm not sure I follow this," Missy said.

"Well, forgive my frankness, but nobody in the class, including us, is exactly a spring chicken. And I think we can assume that none of us has ever killed anybody before."

"Not to my recollection. Except maybe Bob Neufield," Missy said, pushing her hair back out of her eyes and fishing in her purse for her sunglasses.

"Why him in particular?"

"Just because I assume from his manner that he was in the military or law enforcement or one of those immaculately ironed professions. The man has ramrod posture, and his clothes never have so much as a wrinkle. So if he were military, he might have killed someone in war. He's probably old enough to have been in Korea and Vietnam."

"I see what you mean," Jane said. "Did you hear Mrs. Pryce yell something at him about serving his country?"

"Yes. Suggesting that he was a pansy who got thrown out on his ear. Poor guy. He'd been about the only one who'd escaped her nasty tongue, and then she caught him at the end."

"Do you suppose it's true?" Jane asked. "Normally I wouldn't give a damn, but under the circumstances, maybe it's important. Did you tell the police about her saying that?"

"I don't know if it's true, and no, I didn't tell the police. I didn't remember it until now. Listen, Jane, I don't mean to sound callous — I'm truly concerned about this, but I actually came to talk to you about something else, and I don't want it to get lost in this mess. I want to talk to you about your Priscilla project."

"Oh, yes?" Had it suddenly gotten hotter or was it just her nerves coming to life?

Missy looked at her over the top of her sunglasses. "Yes. Let me ask you something — are you having fun doing this or are you just being dutiful about class?"

"I'm having fun. In fact, I'm embarrassed to admit how much fun it is . . ." Jane paused. "No, that's not entirely accurate. I'm enjoying it, but mostly I'm obsessing on it. I guess with two of my kids gone, I need another outlet for that maternal urge to try to run somebody's life. The nice thing about Priscilla is that she has to do what I say. I wouldn't tell this to anybody but you, but even as upset as I was last night, I sat down for a half an hour or so and scribbled a few notes on things I'd thought of for Priscilla to say and do. It's weird, though. I'm not so sure she'll be willing to say and do them —"

Missy nodded. "That's what I'd hoped — and was half-afraid — you'd say. Jane, I don't want to shock you, but I think you're coming down with a book. I know the signs."

"Coming down . . . ? You mean writing a book?" Jane scoffed. "That's ridiculous. I wouldn't have the faintest idea how to write a whole book."

"You write it one page at a time. Just like you're doing."

"No, I'd never consider it. Really."

This whole concept was so revolutionary it almost took her breath away. Could ordinary, real people write books? Missy did. Wow! For a minute it was as if Mrs. Pryce had never existed, much less gotten herself murdered.

"I'm sorry to have to tell you this: You don't get to consider it," Missy was saying. "Writing is something you have to do. An obsession; you use your own word. The world is made up of people who can't write and those who can't help but write. Still, I won't push you. I just wanted to tell you that if you decide to give a serious shot at writing a book, I'd be thrilled to help you."

Willard lumbered to his feet and put a paw on Jane's knee. She absentmindedly fished an ice cube out of her tea and gave it to him. He settled back down, chewing noisily. "Do you mean you think this story of mine really could be a book?" Jane asked.

Missy nodded. "It's remarkably good writing for a beginner. Of course, good writing isn't everything — there's structuring and marketing and a lot more. But good writing *is* the first essential."

They heard the gate squeak, and a moment later Shelley appeared. "Good. You're still here. Mel VanDyne just called me. He said you didn't answer your phone, and asked if I knew what had become of you. I told him I could see you and Missy out here, and he asked everybody to stay put."

"Pitcher of iced tea on the counter," Jane said, feeling this was adequate hostessing for Shelley. She was still trying to cope with what Missy had said.

"Maybe later," Shelley said.

"Not more questions from VanDyne," Missy said. "I'm getting real bored with the few facts I know. It's only a matter of time before I start embroidering them with fictional fillips. Fiction writers are born liars."

Shelley reached toward Jane's glass, which Jane snatched away. "Get your own," she said.

Before Shelley got back, Jane could hear a car door slamming in the driveway. "Around back!" she shouted inelegantly. She was glad that, tired as she was, she'd washed her hair this morning and put on decent clothes. Mel was back in his detective mode, but he might notice her as a woman instead of a peripheral object in an investigation.

He came out onto the patio, holding a glass of tea Shelley had forced on him. She was right behind with the pitcher and a bucket of ice on a tray. Jane wondered how Shelley'd gotten the ice maker to give up its cubes. It tended to create one large, lumpy mass instead of individual pieces. But there wasn't a household appliance in the world that could best Shelley.

Mel sat down with a sigh. The rest of them had at least gotten a few fleeting hours of sleep; Mel must have been up all night. He was wearing the same clothes, but except for the weary sigh, he looked fresh and bright. He repeated what he'd told Jane earlier about Maria Espinoza and the tests. They still didn't have definitive results. "So, ladies, I'd like to go over the food and seating arrangements and so forth with you."

Willard had finished his ice cube and finally noticed there were newcomers. He shambled over to put his head on Mel's thigh. Mel patted his big, square head and waved his hand at the cloud of gnats that went everywhere the dog went.

"We've all been questioned about that already," Missy said. "Can't we go on to something else? It's like revising the same chapter over and over."

"Not until we've got this sorted out. Now, who could have put something in the quiche or the tea?"

Jane sat up straight. "Why the quiche and tea especially?"

"Because that's all the maid had in her stomach. Mrs. Pryce had apparently eaten all kinds of stuff."

"But *I* made the quiche," Jane objected.

"Exactly," he said coolly, staring back at her.

"You don't think *I* poisoned her?"

"As a matter of fact, I don't, but somebody apparently did, and it's my sad job to find out who and how. I have to assume that the quiche itself wasn't poisoned, or other people would have become ill, too. So it must have been put in her food or her drink after she got her plate and cup. Now, where was she sitting? Who could have exchanged her plate or added something to her food?"

"Anybody," Shelley and Missy said together.

Shelley took up the explanation. "The dining room is a very crowded little space, and everybody was crammed together. We were all reaching over and past each other and banging our elbows together. Mrs. Pryce sat at the head of the table with her back to the hallway and kitchen, where the dishes were set out. We had to squeeze past her and each other to get around at all."

"Did she fill her own plate?"

The three women exchanged glances. "I don't think so," Jane finally said. "At least she wasn't in with the lost lemmings."

"I beg your pardon?"

"I mean she wasn't stuffed into the hallway with the rest of us when we were getting our food. At least, I don't think she was."

"Was she at the table when you got there?" Mel asked.

"Yes, and she had a plate full of food. The first time."

"The first time? What?"

"The first time I sat down. But I'd forgotten a drink and —"

Mel held up his hand. "Hold it. Step by step. Where had she gotten the plate if she hadn't filled it herself?"

"I don't know. It was already there when Shelley and I sat down. What about you, Missy?"

Missy had her eyes closed hard. "I'm trying to picture it. I just can't recall. I seem to think I saw someone set it in front of her, but I can't see who. And I'm not sure but what I'm making that up. I don't mean to invent details, it's just that it's my job to do that, and I can't always turn it off."

"I appreciate your honesty," Mel said, looking as if he'd like to shake her teeth loose. "Can you tell me the order that people came to the table?"

"I have no idea," Missy said. "People came, then went and came back again. When I extricated myself from the crowd in the hall — let me see — I think Grady was there already. Yes, he was, because he accidentally bashed a chair leg into me while I was sitting down. And somebody else. I think Ruth Rogers. Or maybe her sister. I wasn't really paying any attention. I was puzzling over some stuff I didn't remember putting on my plate."

"With coconut?" Jane asked. "Somebody gave me a lump of that, too. Maybe — maybe the tea *was* poisoned and there was an antidote in the coconut stuff, and that's why someone made sure we all had some. But then, that can't be, because I didn't eat mine, so I should be dead." She glanced at Mel and realized she was making an ass of herself.

He cleared his throat. "Now that you've reasoned that out, could we continue? You said you left the table —"

"Yes, Mrs. Pryce got snooty about not having a drink, and that made me realize I didn't either. So we all went back — I mean Shelley and I did —"

"And you got Mrs. Pryce's tea?"

"No, I did not," Jane exclaimed. "She went ahead of us and had already gone when Shelley and I got to the kitchen. I think she went around the other way, because when we got back, she stepped on Grady's contact lens. She was coming in the dining room from the other doorway."

"Did she have a cup of tea then?" Mel persisted.

Jane grabbed Willard's collar and dragged him away from Mel, on whose trouser leg he was slobbering. "Sorry about that. I don't know if she had her tea. She probably did. That's what she went to the kitchen for, but I was looking down at Grady and half the others crawling around on the floor. In fact, that would have been a great time to put something on her food. Everybody was looking at Grady. Surely you've questioned everybody else about this."

"Endlessly," Mel said with disgust. "And it sounds like a fire drill in a lunatic asylum. Half this crowd doesn't know where they were, much less where anybody else was at any given moment. Look, I'd like for each of you to write down for me exactly what you did, in what order, and what you can recall of where other people were. In the meantime, I want to talk to you about possible motives."

All three women smiled.

"What? What's funny about motives?"

Shelley broke the news to him. "You'd be hard-pressed to find anyone who had more enemies internationally. There are probably clubs all over the world that meet just to discuss what they'd like to do to her."

Mel slumped in his chair, his gaze shifting slowly from Shelley to Jane. "Someday," he said with great deliberation, "someday when we have lots of time, I'm going to tell you what I think of the people you hang around with, Jane."

— 9 —

"I'm sorry we scared him off before we could talk about motives," Shelley said as the red MG in the driveway roared to life.

"And I'm sorry he left without rescheduling our date," Jane muttered into her iced tea.

"Oh, Jane. I'm sorry," Shelley said. "But you are getting a one-track mind."

"Shelley, it's a track my *mind's* been on for some time. I'm just hoping my body gets a chance to catch up. I've been a widow for some time, you know. I don't mean to be indelicate, but I didn't bury my hormones with Steve, you know."

"You weren't planning to sleep with him at the ice cream store, were you?" Shelley asked bluntly.

"I was hoping to eventually get the opportunity to be asked," Jane said sourly. "The ice cream store seemed a good enough place to get on that path."

Missy gave Jane a sympathetic look.

"Still, it is his job to sort this out. It apparently is murder," Shelley went on.

"What I don't understand," Missy said, "is why anybody *had* to murder her. After all, she was well into her eighties, I would guess. If you really hated her all that much, why not just wait with delicious anticipation for her to die? She was bound to before long. It seems an unnecessary risk to take."

"Obviously someone had to stop her from something she could still do — or say about somebody," Jane said, giving up on the prospect of a juicy discussion of herself and Mel VanDyne. She didn't really want to talk about it anyway — except maybe with him.

"It seems to me that she'd already leveled practically everybody in class." Shelley poured herself some more tea, then she walked over to the fence between Jane's yard and hers and snapped a sprig of mint to pop in her glass.

"Yes, you and Jane are about the only ones she didn't zap," Missy said.

"Which makes us suspects, too. Because she hadn't gotten around to us yet," Shelley said cheerfully.

"Shelley! Are you nuts! I'm the one who made the damned quiche, which is bad enough!" Jane exclaimed. "I think, if anything, somebody was afraid she was going to elaborate on something she'd already started on." She got another ice cube out of her glass and tossed it out into the grass for Willard, hoping he and his gnats would stay out there. He thought it was a game of fetch and brought the ice cube back.

"Like what?"

"Well . . . like her calling Desiree a drunk. Suppose she had some idea that Desiree had done something awful when she was drinking. Running over a kid or something. Not that she did. But Mrs. Pryce didn't seem to care much for the truth of her accusations."

Shelley took up this line of reasoning. "Or her accusations against Grady."

"Grady?" Missy said. "Why Grady? He'd never do anything wrong. He's about the most honest person I've ever met."

"I'm being theoretical," Shelley said patiently. "She'd already started flinging mud at Grady in class about the city's funds. Suppose he was afraid she'd start proclaiming it from the housetops?"

"But Grady *wouldn't* embezzle from anybody."

"That's not the point. I'm sure he wouldn't, but that wouldn't stop her from telling people so. I just mean these things as examples. You know that a false accusation can do as much harm to a person's reputation as a true one. People say where there's smoke, there's fire, and before you know it, the accepted wisdom is that the victim was guilty but just didn't get caught."

"How depressing," Missy said. "Still, I can't imagine Grady Wells as a murderer, and you'll never convince me."

"I wasn't trying to," Shelley said. "I really only meant him as a 'for instance.' Jane, you're being awfully quiet. Are you listening to your hormones again?"

"Huh? Oh, no. I was thinking about the maid. The assumption is that she accidentally or purposely got poisoned by the same person who killed Mrs. Pryce. But what if that person was herself? She could have taken just enough of the poison to get sick, but not die, in order to make everybody think exactly what they are thinking."

"She couldn't have counted on us turning up in time to save her, though."

"So what if we hadn't? There was nothing to keep her from going to the phone and calling for help the minute she thought she was getting in real trouble. For all we knew, she was picking the phone up when we got there."

"But, Jane, unless she was secretly a registered pharmacist, how would she get a deadly poison or know how much was a lethal dose?" Shelley asked.

"I don't know. But we don't know what the poison was. Maybe it's something common for some other use or is common wherever she comes from."

"I don't buy it, but anything's possible," Shelley said. "What's her motive?"

"Motive?" Jane exclaimed. "She was a slave to the dreadful woman. What better motive? Working for Pryce must have been like working for the emotional equivalent of Charles Manson. Think about it: It would be unimaginably horrible actually living with the woman. If you got to the point that you couldn't stand it anymore, you would always know that there'd be a world of other suspects. At any given point in Pryce's life, she could be counted on to have mortally offended at least two or three people within the last week." Jane was really warming to this theory. "If I wanted to kill her, I'd have picked a time and place just like last night — a bunch of her victims all together in her own house. Everybody bringing food that could be poisoned —"

"So you really think the maid did it?" Missy asked.

Jane thought for a minute. "No," she answered, deflated. "I don't, actually. The other side of the coin is that the maid is nearly as old and dotty as Pryce. And now she's out of a job. I'm sure the old harridan didn't make any provisions for her — probably hasn't even been paying her Social Security — and the maid must have known it. Killing Mrs. Pryce would be like killing the goose that laid the golden eggs. The goose might be evil and the eggs tin, but it was better than being old and destitute in a foreign country."

"Scratch the maid," Shelley said.

"What about my theory about Bob Neufield?" Missy asked. She explained to Shelley about her certainty that Neufield was military and might have been discharged for homosexuality.

"Do they do that anymore?" Shelley asked.

"I don't know about now, but he's been living here for ten years or so, I think, and they certainly did then."

Shelley twirled her mint sprig around and mused, "How would she know about it? Pryce, I mean."

"Army, my dear. I imagine the upper echelons are like any other profession — clubby and gossipy. At least writing is that way. I know incredibly personal things about writers I've never met. If Neufield had been high enough ranking, she would have known. For all we know, she was responsible for him being thrown out — if he was."

"Oh —" Jane said.

"Was that the sound of a light going on?" Shelley asked.

"I'm not sure. I sort of flipped through that nasty book of hers, and it seems there was something about leading a drive to have somebody discharged. I didn't really read it, the whole book was so nasty —"

Missy looked horrified. "You know what this could mean, don't you?"

Shelley nodded. "It means we really should read the foul book. I'd rather be a Cub Scout den mother for a year."

"Somebody better give VanDyne a copy," Jane said. "And don't look at me. I won't do it. If I haven't already wrecked my chances with him, that would do it. And we really have to read it, too. Do you have an extra copy, Missy?"

"Extra copy? I must have twenty. She unloaded a whole box of them on me. I guess she thought I'd like to set up a little bookstore and sell them out of the trunk of my car. But I can't read the whole damned thing. I've got a book due in a month, and it would infect my style. I'd be afraid my heroine would turn into a hateful prig. You and Shelley be in charge of searching it for clues."

"I don't know if it'll help anyway," Shelley said. "Except for Bob Neufield, who could she have run into before she lived here?"

"Almost anybody," Jane answered. "My mother knew her. And there are probably others in the class who have lived someplace other than here. I know Desiree lived all over the world as a girl. Anybody could have known her before." She picked a gnat out of her iced tea.

"But she'd have known them, too. She seemed to remember your mom."

"Not until Mother reminded her," Jane pointed out. "Pryce was a very self-absorbed person. And the military's like the State Department. You meet a huge number of people in your life, and you have to have a real gift to remember very many of them."

"Your mother seems to," Missy said.

"She's one of the gifted ones. That's why she's such an asset to my father's work. I suspect their postings nowadays have as much to do with her skills as his."

"Oh? What else is she good at?" Missy asked.

"Everything," Jane said sourly.

"Aha. Do I detect a case of PMS?"

"What's PMS have to do with it?" Jane asked.

"Perfect Mother Syndrome," Missy answered. "I suffered from it for years. When I was growing up, my school friends would come to my house to see my mother — not me. She was so damned perfect. Understanding, funny, beautiful —"

Jane nodded. "And knowing it was stupid because you knew you ought to be grateful because everyone else your age hated their mothers?"

"Absolutely —"

Shelley cleared her throat and, in her best president-of-the-PTA voice, said, "Ladies, I believe we're wandering from the point — somebody in our neighborhood, in the class Missy intends to continue, is a murderer. Or have you both forgotten?"

"Yes, yes. You're right," Missy admitted. "But we've eliminated Grady and Bob Neufield and the maid. I assume we're eliminating ourselves and Jane's mother."

"We certainly are!" Jane said emphatically.

"So who does that leave? Desiree Loftus and the biblical sisters, or whatever Desiree calls them."

"Pretty slim pickings," Shelley said. "Desiree is outrageous but good-hearted, and Ruth and Naomi — well, I'm always surprised that they do all that gardening; I can't picture either of them having the heart to kill the insect pests."

"As for Desiree, Pryce really hated her, but she seemed to take it as a great joke," Jane said. "She told me once that she took a certain pride in who disliked her. She seemed to get a kick out of goading Mrs. Pryce."

"I don't know," Shelley said. "That remark about her drinking seemed to set her back a bit. Only for a moment, but it might have hit a sensitive nerve."

"Does she really drink, or is she just eccentric?" Missy asked.

"Oh, I think she drinks," Jane said. "She distills stuff in her basement. Or ferments it or something. At least she's given it a shot. I was collecting for a charity one day and she invited me in to see. Naomi Smith had told her how to make a foul concoction of nasturtium buds or something, and she wanted me to try it out. It was supposed to be wine, but it was like drinking Lysol with suspicious bits of sludge in it."

"Then she could make poison in her basement, couldn't she?" Shelley asked.

"I don't think so. She didn't seem to have a grip on how to make anything," Jane said. "It was probably just one of her passing enthusiasms. Remember when she tried to build her own solar panels on her roof? The city stopped her because they were afraid all that gravel was going to avalanche off and kill somebody."

"Then there was the time she decided to have a southwest garden," Missy reminded them. "She had all her grass scraped off and put in rocks and cacti. Nobody could convince her that the first freeze was going to turn the cacti to mush. It must have cost her the earth to have the sodden things and all the boulders hauled off and the grass put back."

"Money . . ." Jane said. "Maybe it's about money. Mrs. Pryce's murder. Most crimes are, I think. Do you think maybe there's something terribly valuable in all that junk in her house, and maybe her children wanted to inherit it? There were some really nice things in with the junk. Her family has waited a long time already. Maybe they just got tired of biding their time." Jane shifted her chair to get out of the sun, which was becoming uncomfortably warm. They really should go inside, but Jane hated being cooped up indoors.

"Jane, I hate to be the one to point out the obvious, but none of her children are in our class," Shelley said.

"That we know of," Jane said. "Her children would be in their sixties, and her grandchildren maybe in their forties. She could have a grandchild she doesn't even know by sight. She was probably on terrible terms with her family. It wouldn't be surprising if she were estranged from all of them. She never mentioned family. Did you notice that there were no pictures of people in her house? I think that's what made it all so depressing. There was nothing human there. Just stuff."

Missy started gathering up her purse and car keys and sunglasses. "I think what we've done today is significant. It appears that we've proved that nobody could have killed her, and the whole episode was just a particularly revolting illusion."

Jane laughed. "I love it when you talk like a writer."

As Missy was getting up, Denise Nowack came out into her backyard, wearing a big picture hat that not only concealed her hair, but muffled her voice. "Mom!" she yelled. "There's a man on the phone saying will Mrs. Jeffry please go in her house and answer her phone?"

— 10 —

"Jane? It's Mel. Sorry I left so abruptly."

"Have you slept since yesterday?" she asked, then mentally chided herself for automatically going into her mother mode. He was a grown man, and if he didn't get enough rest, it was his problem.

"A little. Could you have lunch with me?"

Jane smiled. "Business or pleasure?"

"Business, I'm afraid."

The smile faded.

"Then we want to talk quietly. How about coming here?" As she spoke, she was frantically taking a mental inventory of the fridge. She'd have to make a flying trip to the grocery store.

"Quietly? At your house? Jane, that's like trying to have a cozy chat in the middle of a four-alarm fire."

He probably lives in a hermetically sealed, professionally soundproofed luxury apartment — with white carpets and a doorman to keep away unwanted visitors, she thought. We're worlds apart. "Okay, whatever you say. Noon?"

"That's fine. I'll pick you up."

Shelley came to the kitchen door a minute later. "I accidentally went home with your glass. Here. It was VanDyne calling, wasn't it?"

"Yes, asking me to lunch. As a suspect, I think."

"Jane, the police don't ask suspects to lunch. God! Your hair. What can we do to it by lunchtime?"

"Nothing. Shelley, I've made a grown-up decision. If Mel VanDyne's interested in me at all, it's as an example of a species: Housewifius Domesticus. I might as well look the part. It's what I am."

"That's pitiful-sounding."

"No, it's the truth. We don't have a thing in common."

"He's a man and you're a woman. That's enough."

"He's a quintessential yuppie and I'm a happy frump with stretch marks."

"You know what you need?"

"What?" Jane asked suspiciously. "A night on the town? My boobs jacked up? A new perm?"

"A job."

Jane sat down at the kitchen table and motioned Shelley to join her. "That's the last thing I expected you to say. You interest

118

me strangely," she said. "Explain."

"Well, we're a dying breed — mothers who are just mothers. Look at this neighborhood. Every year it gets quieter during the day. Everybody's off doing something that makes them feel like more than just a housewife."

"You're right about all that, but none of it has to do with why I need a job. I need the money."

"Jane — is there something I can help with?"

Jane smiled. "No. Thanks, Shelley, but it's not that I'm desperate. I can pay for insurance and food and school clothes and all the necessities. I'm really lucky that way. Most single mothers haven't got it so good. But it's the extras that really aren't so extra. My car's falling to bits; my clothes are all ratty and out of fashion. Even the bath towels are getting shot. I priced some new ones last week, and they cost the earth. Mike needs a new tuba; his was about sixth-hand and we got it cheap, meaning to get him a good one if he kept up with his playing."

"You've got that money your friend left in her will."

"Yes, and I'm keeping it for myself like you told me I had to. I wouldn't dare defy one of your edicts. But I don't want to just spend it on stuff like towels. I want to use it for something important — I just don't know what that is yet."

"Investing in a business of your own?"

"Something like that. But what would I do? Mothering's what I do pretty well, and without a father, my kids deserve a full-time mother. I don't want to be like my mom."

"What's wrong with being perfect?" Shelley asked with a grin.

Jane sighed. "My mother was a perfect wife, not a perfect mother."

"I thought they usually went together."

"Yes, usually. I could only say this to a real friend. . . . My mother has always adored my father. They didn't need my sister and me to make a family. They are a family all by themselves. All the time I was growing up, we did what was best for his career, even though it meant we never stayed anywhere long enough to feel at home. My sister and I never went two years in a row to the same school, or even in the same country. I resented that. And I never realized how much until I was grown."

"But that was because of what he did for a living, Jane. Would you have rather your mother stayed behind somewhere with you?"

"God, no. I just never felt like I came first with her. If I got sick and there was an important embassy party, she'd get a nurse to stay with me, but she'd go to the party because it was important to my father's career."

"Hiring a nurse isn't exactly neglectful," Shelley said softly.

"Oh, Shelley, I don't mean I was neglected. I know that in most ways I was very lucky. You can't tell me anything sensible I haven't told myself. See, you're sitting here talking to 'Jane Jeffry, semi-intelligent adult.' But the person who's doing this whining is little Janie Grant, a selfish child who wants, just once, to have her mommy's *full* attention. That's why I feel so strongly that I can't take on anything that would take my attention away from my kids. I don't want to be like her."

"I understand. I think you could do with a shrink, but I do understand. But what about all those hours of the year that the kids are at school and don't need your attention or even want it?"

"You know that time is busy. You do what I do with it — cook, clean, run car pools, do civic stuff. I've got my blind kids I drive once a week —"

"But your own kids can learn to help

121

cook, you could hire help to clean if you had extra income. Mike can drive now and could take up part of the car-pooling if you'd let Thelma get him a car like she keeps threatening. If you had a part-time job, or a job at home, you could still do a lot of your other things. Jane, it wouldn't hurt them a bit to be more responsible at home."

"You've thought about this a lot, haven't you?" Jane asked.

"On my own behalf, I assure you."

"You're going to work?"

"I'm thinking about helping Paul with the franchises in some way." Shelley's husband was a type-A second-generation Pole who owned a chain of Greek fast-food restaurants.

"But you've got a built-in employer who won't care if you've got to stay home with somebody with measles or take off a day to work on the PTA carnival."

"Yes, but so have you, come to that. There's Steve's family's pharmacies. You've worked there before."

Jane held up her forefingers in a cross shape. "Work for Thelma? Have you gone completely insane? It's bad enough having her for a mother-in-law."

"Maybe you're right."

"In any case, my job right now involves

getting Katie up and moving. Thanks for listening to my selfish whimpering."

"What are friends for?" Shelley said.

Mel VanDyne showed up on the dot of one with a picnic lunch in paper sacks from a chic catering shop. They drove a few blocks to a city park and staked out a picnic table as far as possible from a raucous softball game. He took four bottled wine coolers from a little insulated bag.

"Where's the rest of your family?" he asked politely as he unwrapped pricey little crustless sandwiches and individual plastic cups of pasta salad.

"My oldest son is looking at colleges with a friend, my youngest is on a trip with his grandmother, Katie's at work, and my mom's visiting a friend," Jane reeled off, proud of resisting the urge to elaborate on these domestic arrangements. Now that she'd decided to give up trying to impress him, she felt much more comfortable around him.

"So tell me about the people at the dinner."

So much for small talk.

Jane quickly summarized the discussion she'd had earlier in the day with Shelley and Missy. "We don't know anything about her

123

family, of course. Or about the maid."

"We've done some checking," he said, unwrapping plastic forks and handing one to her. "According to the maid, there's only one child still living, a son who was in plumbing fixtures who's retired to Arizona. The two daughters, both deceased, each left children and grandchildren. They're scattered all over the country. There was a safe in the house. Presumably a will in it, but we haven't found the combination yet. We're hoping that the obit notice in the paper will bring out a lawyer. The maid didn't know who that might be, and she's not well enough to question thoroughly. There was a checkbook in the desk showing a balance of close to twenty thousand dollars, so there might be money involved."

"What about the maid?"

"She's in pretty bad shape. Not much question of poisoning herself, although it's possible. She could have misjudged a dosage." At Jane's surprised look, he said, "We do think of these things, too."

"What about the poison? What was it?"

"We don't know yet. The path lab is doing tests for the usual — arsenic, strychnine, digitalis. But these tests take longer than anyone likes to admit, and they haven't come up with anything yet. There are about

124

a thousand weird things that are poisonous, and it takes a while to test for each one. And it's complicated by the fact that Mrs. Pryce was so old. At her age, a lot of systems have failed or are failing on their own. Also, it could have taken a virtually indetectable amount of some poisons to push her and the maid over. Maria Espinoza says she's seventy-nine and Pryce was eighty-seven, and they both had bad hearts. It could have been something that would only make you and me a little bit sick, but was deadly to them."

"But the murderer must have known that. Doesn't that narrow the field to people who knew them well enough to gauge the dosage?"

"Not necessarily. The killer could have just used something at hand and hoped like hell that it would work. Maybe it wasn't even meant to kill her. Just to make her sick as a 'punishment.' "

"Could it have been in her house? In a prescription?"

"Unlikely. A lot of things that are poisonous in large amounts are used in minute portions for medication. But you'd have to eat a bowlful of pills. It was in the quiche or the tea. More accurately, in Mrs. Pryce's quiche or tea. The maid didn't serve herself, she just ate and drank what was left of her employer's food. I guess it was a habit of hers. She says she had a bite or two of the quiche, but thought it tasted strange and left the rest. Unfortunately, she'd already put all the plates in the dishwasher and run them through by the time we got there."

"Why didn't Pryce taste it?"

"I don't know, except the pathologist says some elderly people lose their sense of taste. Or maybe she was just a glutton who didn't care."

"Oh, she cared. She made nasty remarks about every dish in front of her. She said there was too much mayonnaise in the potato salad and too much oil on the green salad, and Missy's cake was too dry. But those are texture things, not taste, I guess. And it seemed she put away a lot of food in spite of her complaints."

"Run through what she'd come down on everybody about again, would you?" Mel said. "Aren't you going to eat that sandwich?"

He'd managed to wolf down his share of the dainty edibles. "I'll give you half," Jane said. While she wasn't very hungry, she'd heard great things about the caterer he'd gotten this stuff from, and didn't want to miss her chance to at least taste their work. "Let's see — she accused my mother of being an embassy hanger-on, which is a really nasty remark from an insider. She called Desiree a drunk and Grady at embezzler and Missy a pornographer. She wouldn't sit by Naomi Smith because she was afraid Naomi would give her some disease, and at the end she made a crack about Bob Neufield being too depraved to serve his country."

Mel was taking notes with one hand and eating with the other. "Uh-huh. So she didn't go after you or your friend Shelley or Ruth Rogers."

"Yet, you mean?" Jane asked, thinking about Shelley's theory that they were better suspects because they might have killed her to keep her from getting around to them.

"Not exactly," he said around the last bite of her pasta salad, which he'd liberated without her noticing. "I'm just trying to get a relative fix on this. Embezzlement's a pretty strong accusation. Thinking somebody's going to give you a cold is nothing."

"Oh, but it's not a cold. Mrs. Pryce accused Naomi of having cancer and asked her to move. Ruth Rogers came tearing in and told her off. Said her sister had a rare blood disease that wasn't contagious."

"Still, it's rude as hell, but not really damaging. Not like accusing the mayor of stealing the city's money."

"I agree, but when you get to know Grady, you'll know how crazy the accusation is. He's a really nice man."

He looked at her pityingly. "Jane, really nice people have embezzled money. The two are not mutually exclusive."

"But I don't *want* it to be Grady — or anybody in the class!" Jane said.

"No? But it was, and I don't want anybody to get away with it. Do you?"

It was a stupid question and it made her mad. "Why did you ask me out yesterday?" Jane asked, surprising him with the question only slightly more than she surprised herself.

"Why . . . ? I don't know. To apologize for disappearing. To see how you were. To thank you for Christmas dinner —"

"Out of duty?" she asked.

"No!" he snapped. He started gathering up the paraphernalia of lunch and stuffing it into an empty sack. "But I've got a duty right now, and I better get back to it. Are you through?" His voice was cold and formal.

"It appears I am," she said, taking a bite of the sandwich she'd managed to save from his cleanup. It was so trendily wholesome that it tasted like sawdust with a little basil.

It was probably just as well that he'd hogged hers.

They got in the car and rode silently. As Mel pulled into her driveway, he said, "Sorry about that. I'm tired, and murder pisses me off. Do I get another chance? How about a late dinner tonight after your class?"

"On two conditions."

"Yeah? What are they?" he asked suspiciously.

"You take a nap first, and you keep your greedy hands off my food."

Mel grinned.

Jane stood in the driveway and watched as he drove off, thinking that he'd said something profound. Murder pissed her off, too. On the surface of her life, she'd taken Mrs. Pryce's death rather lightly. Partly because Pryce was such a dreadful person; partly because Jane herself was so preoccupied with her mother's visit and the story she was working on about Priscilla. But underneath, she was extremely distressed.

Murder was wrong; there was no provocation sufficient to justify it. And Jane was of the belief that killing someone was one of those horrible hurdles that, once taken, became easier. For the first time, she consciously realized that someone in the class was dangerous to all of them for that reason.

But when the class was over in a few days, they'd all go their separate ways, meeting only casually at the dry cleaner's and the grocery store. And if that person had gotten away with murder, it would be harder to unravel the truth.

This crime would be much easier to figure out now rather than later. Mel and the police weren't making any progress, for all their technical inventory. This wasn't one of those cases where there were blood samples and fingerprints to analyze. This was very personal; a neighborhood crime that would have to be solved in the neighborhood, not in a crime lab.

— 11 —

When Jane came in the door, the phone was ringing. It was Ruth Rogers. "Jane, your mother seems such a lovely, interesting person, and there's never much time to visit with each other in class. Might the two of you be free this afternoon for tea?"

"Ruth, how nice. I'd love it, but I'll have to check that Mom doesn't have any plans."

Cecily had just come into the kitchen with a towel on her head. "Sounds great," she said when Jane explained.

"Why don't you come by around three?" Ruth said.

This arranged, Jane hung up. "I didn't know you were here," she said to Cecily. "How was lunch with your friend?"

"Fine, except that I'm getting to the age that my contemporaries all want to talk about who's died lately. It's depressing. I resisted telling her about Mrs. Pryce's death. Harriet didn't know her and wouldn't have appreciated the justice in it. I put your car in the garage and the keys on the dining room table." Cecily gave her hair a final rub, took the towel to the guest bath just off the kitchen, and came back, running her fingers through her damp curls. Jane felt a surge of feminine resentment that this was all her mother had to do to look smashing. She mentioned this.

Cecily sat down at the kitchen table, smiling. "I've always been sorry that you girls got your father's hair. But then, you got my strong teeth and my feet. We have adorable little feet, don't we? You could have inherited his feet and had to wear gunboats for shoes. That was the detective you were out with, wasn't it? Do the police know any more yet?"

"Not much." She told her mother what he'd said about the difficulty of determining what the poison was. "Mainly he asked me about the people in the class."

"It's such a shame that it happened like it did. I don't suppose there's a shred of a chance that it was someone outside that small group."

"I don't see how. The maid got sick from eating what was left on Mrs. Pryce's plate, so her food had to contain the poison. And since it was the same food we all had, someone had to have put it on her plate while we were all milling around, trying to get served and seated — or while the search for Grady's contact lens was going on."

"But who? Everybody there seems like perfectly ordinary, nice people. How well do you know all of them?"

"Most of them between slightly and fairly well. I only know Bob Neufield by sight. I don't know a thing about him except that he's an occasional Friend of the Library volunteer. He lets himself get pressed into service when there are cartons of books to haul to the mall for the annual Friends Book Sale. As for Grady, I've met him several times at neighborhood picnics and city council things. He has a company that makes playing cards, and he's always making commemorative ones for people and giving them away. Anniversaries, birthdays, the town's founding. He's very generous and well liked. He's single. Rumor has it that he was married once, but his wife died young."

Cecily nodded. "What about the exotic gal in the caftan and sandals?"

"Desiree Loftus. I run into her every month or so someplace. She seems to have a lot of money from some mysterious source. Always indulging herself in weird causes and trying to preach them to anybody who'll listen. Cryogenics. Miracle diets. Nudism. Stuff like that."

"What about the ladies we're having tea with?"

"Ruth Rogers is a fixture here. Been around forever. She used to baby-sit the kids sometimes when they were babies. Wouldn't let me pay her. Said she loved little children. She used to be a nursery school teacher, she said, and missed it."

"What about her sister?"

"Naomi's lived here for a couple years. I haven't seen much of her; she's sick a lot of the time. She was taken off in an ambulance about six months ago — you can just see the end of their driveway from my kitchen window. She's had a very hard life, I understand. They found each other through some lost relative bureau. I think they're both widowed. Somebody told me Naomi has an impressive cookbook collection. Valuable antique ones, I mean. Or maybe it's Ruth with the collection. I'm not sure."

"What about the teacher? Missy," Cecily asked. "Every time I look at her, she reminds me of somebody, and for the life of me, I can't figure out who."

"John Cleese?"

Cecily's eyes opened very wide and she started laughing. "God! You're right. I'm sorry you told me!"

"Don't worry. She knows it. I understand

she can sometimes be persuaded to do the *'Dead Parrot'* routine at parties. Missy's a terrific person. She has a husband somewhere. She once said they hadn't seen each other for ten years, but never got divorced because they both felt one marriage was more than enough. At least, that's what she said. I believe she's Catholic, so maybe that's the real reason they didn't divorce. She used to write textbooks for English classes, but writes romance novels now. She says it pays better."

Willard had laid his head on Cecily's leg and was giving her longing looks. Cecily got up, gave him a treat from his plastic box on the counter, and let him out the kitchen door.

"Still, if we can assume you and I and Shelley are innocent," she said, "it means one of those nice people killed Mrs. Pryce and nearly killed her maid," she said.

"Come in, come in," Ruth Rogers said. She'd dressed for tea in a pale blue dress with flowing sleeves and the inevitable ruffles. She wore what Jane's mother often called "daytime pearls." Jane was glad that her instinct had told her to dress up in a skirt and ruffled white blouse for Ruth's tea party. "I'm so glad you could take time from your visit to come by. Mrs. Grant — may I call you Cecily? I feel I know you from your class project."

"Yes, please," Cecily replied.

"And I'm Ruth. My sister and I have so much enjoyed reading the first chapters of the autobiographies. Especially yours. What a very interesting life you've had. Jane, aren't you writing your life?"

"No, I've invented one, but I haven't let anybody but Missy see it."

"What a splendid idea! Naomi will be down in a moment. She's feeling a little puny today and just woke from a nap. Would you like to see the garden? It's hot out, but we wouldn't be long."

"You and Mother go. I'd just be eaten up with jealousy," Jane said. "I've got my first garden, and between the pets and the bugs, it's a pitiful thing."

"Organic pest control. That's the key. I'll send some articles home with you. Now, Cecily, I've got some daylilies I want you to see. . . ."

Their voices trailed off. Jane looked around the room. It was extremely feminine without being fussy. Most of the furniture was ornate but delicate antiques; little pie-crust tables, a pair of Empire love seats with tapestry upholstery by the fireplace. Jane thought the color of the fabric was probably ashes of roses, a description that had always fascinated her. In front of the fireplace was a lovely peacock feather fan. Off the living room was a room that looked as if it had once been a porch, but was now enclosed to form a combination sun room/greenhouse. Light streamed in the windows that completely surrounded it. There were lush African violets on the windowsills and airy ferns hanging from the ceiling. The furniture was fresh white wicker with plump floral cushions. It was definitely a woman's house. Jane wondered if it had been like this when Ruth's husband was living or whether Ruth and Naomi had gradually made it over to suit their tastes.

Naomi came in the room as Jane was studying a china shepherdess on the mantel. "Oh, Jane. I didn't hear you come in. Ruth should have told me. Is she showing off the garden?"

"Yes, to my mother. Is that your cookbook collection?" Jane asked, gesturing toward a bookshelf of old books next to the fireplace.

"Why, yes. I've made scones for our tea from one of them. Would you like to see some of my favorites?"

Some of the books weren't even really

books anymore, just sets of loose pages with ribbons and strings keeping them together. Others were so formidably bound that Jane found herself wondering about the strength of the women who'd first acquired them. Most were published works, but some of the oldest were handmade to pass from mother to daughter, often with drawings and sketches to illustrate methods of preparing and cooking. Naomi not only collected the books, she tried most of the recipes to the best of her ability — given directions like "churn until curdled" and "take a two-month-old piglet . . ." She promised to copy down some of the best recipes for Jane.

"My very favorite is a recipe for relish from a Victorian-era book. The author says to season until 'it's as sharp as a mother-in-law's tongue, and use in very small portions,' " Naomi said with a laugh. Jane liked the way Naomi handled the fragile old books — with care, but not fanatic care. In her hands, they weren't just objects of historical merit, but old friends.

"Oh, you've shown off your books without Cecily here," Ruth chided, coming back into the room with Jane's mother in tow. "Now you'll have to do it again. Ladies, do sit down while I get the tea."

Naomi ran through a few of the high

138

points and had just retold the relish story when Ruth backed through the kitchen door, balancing a huge silver tray. Naomi tried to help her, but Ruth said the tray was far too heavy for her. She set it down on a low coffee table.

Jane's eyes nearly bulged at the sight of the food on the tray. There was a plate of tiny sandwiches cut in fancy shapes with a cookie cutter and sprinkled with a dusting of parsley, another piled high with scones, a bowl of what she later learned was sweet clotted cream. The tea steaming in a small silver tea urn was strong Earl Grey. It was accompanied by tiny bowls of colored sugar. To finish, there were fragrant puff pastries with crushed nuts in a gooey candied syrup over the tops. And tucked among all the dishes were sprigs of rosemary and several tiny glass vials with delicate brilliant yellow flowers and fragile, pungent foliage. "Dahlberg daisies," Ruth explained. "They grow like weeds, and most people don't even know about them."

Jane could hardly speak. The look, the smell — heaven!

While they ate, Ruth and Naomi frankly bragged on each other, Ruth complimenting Naomi's cooking, and Naomi boasting about Ruth's gardening, particularly an iris that Ruth had developed and named for her late husband. When Ruth referred to Naomi as her "little sister," Jane was surprised. Naomi, frail and ill, looked a good ten years older than the robust, tanned Ruth.

"Missy told me the two of you are planning to write a joint autobiography," Jane said when she finally reached the point that she could stop gobbling and talk. She felt as if she could just tuck in her arms and legs and roll home. "Why didn't you turn it in to the class?"

"Each of us has written a large portion of our own, but the problem is in how to join the two," Ruth said. "That's why we were so anxious to take Missy's class. Alternating chapters seems obvious, but I think would be confusing unless one of them is cast in the third person. And of course, there's very little logical overlap. We didn't find each other until so recently."

"Yet you seem like you've been together forever," Cecily said, daintily sucking a little syrup off her fingertip. "How did you get separated, if you don't mind my asking?"

"No, not at all. It was a long time ago. Our parents both died during the war — World War Two, which seems a thousand years ago now. I was only six, and Naomi was a baby," Ruth explained, giving her sister a quick smile. Naomi returned the smile, but shakily. Jane was uneasy, but certainly Ruth wouldn't be telling this story unless she and Naomi had come to terms with it.

"Things were so confused," Ruth went on. "We had only one relative — an uncle who'd died in Germany. We were shipped off from the South Pacific to his widow in Detroit, a young show girl who was appalled to have us dumped on her. She just gave us away like you would puppies. We each drifted from family to family. I was very fortunate to end up with a childless couple — a professor and his wife. Naomi wasn't so lucky. Naomi, darling, don't you think you might go up and lie down a bit?" she broke off.

Naomi had grown even paler, and her fingers were like claws on the arms of the chair.

"Excuse me," Naomi said. "I think I will. But I'll see you in class tonight. Maybe we can meet again before you have to leave," she said to Cecily. Her voice was thin and weak.

When she'd gone, Cecily said, "I'm sorry if we upset her by asking."

"Oh, no. It's not that at all. It's just that

she has to have regular blood transfusions, and she's a little overdue. The doctors have recently adjusted her medication, too, and she's been awfully tired the last couple days."

"It's a shame Mrs. Pryce was so rude to her about her illness," Jane said.

"Terrible. I'm afraid I overreacted. It's amazing how many times something like that has happened, however. Most people are more subtle about it, but it's a health-conscious world, and people are terrified to be around someone seriously ill. Naomi's more philosophical about it than I am. She jumped all over me for making a scene." But for all her calm appraisal, she looked worried and glanced once or twice over her shoulder as she spoke, obviously concerned with whether her sister had gotten up the stairs safely.

"We're going to get out of your way," Cecily said, standing suddenly and moving toward the door at a pace that was courteous and yet brooked no argument.

"Could I ask you a favor, Jane?" Ruth said. "Are you going out anywhere this afternoon?"

"Yes, I have to take Katie a sandwich for her dinner."

"That's wonderful. Would you drop this

sign-up sheet at Bob Neufield's on the way? He lives right across from the pool. I was supposed to take it this morning, but I was concerned about Naomi and just forgot. Naomi had a little dizzy spell that shook me up. This list is for the library sale, and I've held it up too long."

Jane leaped at the chance. She wanted to talk to Bob Neufield, just to get to know him a little better. It was an impulse she was sure Mel VanDyne would disapprove of, but the police were making so little headway, and it was possible she could learn something that could unravel the mystery of Mrs. Pryce's death.

"Aren't they interesting women?" Cecily said as they headed for home. "So fond of each other and so proud of each other's interests."

Jane smiled and glanced sideways at her. "Wishing you had daughters like that? Maybe if you'd kept us apart for a few decades . . . Still, I'll call Marty next week. Promise. And I won't even mention her cretin of a husband."

"Somehow, I think you're missing the point."

They got in the house, and Cecily yawned and said, "That nap idea sounds good. Do you mind . . . ?"

"Not in the least." As soon as her mother was out of earshot, Jane dialed the phone. "Shelley, want to do a little snooping? I've got a legitimate excuse to go by Bob Neufield's. Just give me time to pack a sandwich."

"You're taking Bob Neufield a sandwich?"

"No, the sandwich is for Katie. Seven minutes tops."

— 12 —

Shelley was waiting in her minivan in her driveway when Jane dashed out with Katie's hastily assembled sack dinner. "Mother and I just had tea with Ruth and Naomi," she said, snapping the seat belt and testing that it was secure. With Shelley at the wheel, it wasn't an idle activity. She'd have felt better with a crash helmet as well.

"Learn anything helpful?" Shelley asked, backing out at the speed of sound. Shelley was a very polite, ladylike person, but all her aggressions came out when she was driving.

"Not much," Jane admitted, her foot pressed so hard to an imaginary brake pedal that her muscles cramped. She always told herself she'd be better off if she just closed her eyes and imagined she was on the Concorde, but she couldn't do it. "Mostly negative as far as the murder goes. I mentioned to Ruth how nasty it was of Mrs. Pryce to act like Naomi was contagious, and Ruth said lots of people have done the same thing, mostly in slightly nicer ways."

"You're kidding!"

"Watch the road, Shelley!"

"I've never had an accident," Shelley said with haughty dignity. "So much for Naomi killing her because she was hurt and insulted."

"It never was a good motive," Jane said.

"I know. If we went around killing people who insulted us, there'd be nobody left at the phone company or the IRS. What about Ruth? Was she mad enough to have done something on Naomi's behalf?"

"Maybe at the moment, but she said Naomi read her the riot act afterwards. Ruth even admitted she overreacted. I can't see a sudden rage lasting until the next day. Especially when the victim of the insult wasn't that upset. Well, upset, but resigned anyway."

"I don't suppose the subject of poisons came up?"

Jane could have sworn Shelley took the last turn on two of the van's four wheels. "Hardly. That would have been like saying, thanks for the lovely tea, and by the way, have you murdered anyone lately?"

"Nonsense. It was a logical thing to mention."

"I guess so, but I didn't get a chance. Although, in a way, it *did* come up. Ruth pressed some articles on me about organic gardening. She's real high on it. That probably means she doesn't have any garden poisons around. Anyway, there was lots of chitchat, then Naomi started feeling bad, so we got out."

"Organic gardening," Shelley mused, narrowly missing a parked car.

"It was mainly about compost and using Ivory Liquid to kill aphids," Jane explained. "I don't think you could kill anyone with compost — unless you buried them in it."

Shelley screeched to a stop in front of the pool. "What else did you talk about?"

"Honk for Katie," Jane said, then proceeded to repeat as much of the conversation as she could remember while they waited for Katie to notice them.

"I don't see anything dark and mysterious in any of that," Shelley mused. She made it sound as if it were Jane's fault.

Katie came bouncing over to the car. "Hi, Mrs. Nowack. Thanks, Mom. It's not peanut butter again, is it?"

"No, it's cream cheese with pineapple," Jane said placidly. Katie looked stricken. "Just kidding. It's roast beef and pickles."

"Good. See ya."

When they were off again, Shelley said, "Didn't Ruth used to be a nurse? Maybe she could get poisons from the hospital."

"Hold it. That's the house. No, she

wasn't a nurse. She was a nursery school teacher. I doubt that she had contact with anything more dangerous than peroxide for cuts there."

"Jane, you're not cooperating. We've got to figure out who did this. Anybody could be the next victim."

"I want to know just as much as you do. I'm just pointing out that you can't pin it on Ruth because she was a nurse when she wasn't one. Boy, is that ever a bachelor's house," she added, gazing out at Bob Neufield's plain, boxy home.

The house was sparkling white and the lawn excruciatingly tidy, but the whole had a naked, unfinished look. There were no shutters to frame the windows and give a contrast of color, no foundation plantings, no flowers, not even a rail around the cement slab porch. The windows on the front didn't even have curtains, only utilitarian roller shades.

"Now, that's a man who needs a dozen plastic flamingos to dress the place up," Jane said with a giggle, then immediately sobered when she remembered the purpose of their visit. "Now, Shelley, don't ask anything too blunt."

"What do you mean? I'm the soul of tact."

"I just mean we want to figure this out, but

we don't want to put ourselves in danger. No 'what were you doing the night of blah blah' stuff that makes us sound like detectives."

They left the car on the street under a shade tree and went to the door. There wasn't a doorbell, so they knocked.

Bob Neufield opened the door and stared at them for a moment, obviously trying to place them.

"Mr. Neufield, I'm Jane Jeffry and this is Shelley Nowack. We're in Missy's class with you."

"Oh, yes. Sorry." He smiled, but it was the expression of a man who'd been told it was courteous to smile and didn't quite know why he should.

Jane waited a few seconds for him to step aside and invite them in, but he didn't. "Ruth Rogers asked me to drop off a sign-up sheet for some library thing." She handed it to him.

He took it, glanced at the heading, and said, "Thanks."

There was another awkward pause. Shelley said, "If you're not busy, I wonder if we could come in for a moment."

Count on Shelley, Jane thought.

Neufield looked perplexed, but said, "Sure. Come in."

The living room was like the front of the

house: painfully neat, but with nothing to suggest real human habitation. The walls were bare of pictures. The furniture was of nice quality, but it looked as if it were set up for a catalog photograph. Everything was shades of tasteful, boring beige. There was a bookshelf, but it contained only books. Very few pictures or ornaments or memorabilia. Only a football trophy and one intriguing picture of a beautiful young woman. "I see you're interested in military history," Jane said, scanning a few of the book titles.

"Yes, it's been a lifelong hobby of mine. I've even had a few articles published in some of the history magazines," he said, apparently mistaking Jane's comment for passionate interest. "I have quite a collection of artifacts, too. Would you like to see them?"

"We'd love to," Jane said, looking smugly at Shelley as if to say, 'See? I can get people to talk.'

He led them down a hallway off the living room, past a bedroom, bathroom, and into the back of the house. This had probably been two good-sized rooms originally. The dividing wall had been knocked out, making the entire width of the house into a single huge area. Unlike the rest of the house, this space was full of objects. Guns, sabers, and shields covered the walls. Glass-topped tables were full of knives. Cabinets were open to display helmets, cannonballs, field surgical kits, and bits of military harnesses. In a quick visual sweep, Jane spotted several grenades, a number of weapons that looked as if they belonged to modern terrorists, and what appeared to be a machine gun, sitting on top of a desk and pointed out the back window. Studying the window, she noticed a thin black line in the glass. An alarm system.

She and Shelley gazed about in stupefaction before Jane managed to croak, "This is a stunning collection, Mr. Neufield."

"Thank you. I collect primarily World War One, but I've gotten interested lately in Civil War, and a number of very good pieces have come on the market with the recession."

"What's this?" Shelley asked of an object on the table next to the door.

"A canister of mustard gas."

"Oh!" she said, jerking her hand back and moving away.

"Probably inert by now, but I've never wanted to find out," he said, with a short bark of a laugh. "You ladies are welcome to look around as much as you like, but if we're going to stay in here, I need to keep the door closed. Humidity control, you see." He was

151

looking at an elaborate set of gauges on the wall next to the door as he spoke.

"Oh, we wouldn't want to mess things up," Jane said hastily. The room and its keeper made her uneasy, and she wasn't about to be locked up in it. Bob looked so disappointed that they stayed a little longer, trying to pretend an interest other than terror. Finally Jane guessed they'd stayed long enough to keep from hurting his feelings. "Well, this is truly a remarkable collection," she said, moving toward the doorway.

They went back to the living room, and Bob Neufield said, "Would you like some coffee?" Again, it was as if he'd been told this was part of the script of a play he didn't quite understand.

"We wanted to talk to you about Mrs. Pryce's death. It was almost surely murder, you know," Jane said.

Shelley shot her a surprised look, as if to say, "Where were you on the night of blah blah."

He nodded. "So I was led to believe. What do you want to talk about it for?"

"To see if we can't figure it out," Shelley said, casting caution entirely to the winds.

"Why would you do that?" he asked, genuinely puzzled.

The two women looked at each other in confusion. "Don't you want the killer caught, Mr. Neufield?" Jane asked.

"Of course I do, but it's the job of the police to figure it out, and the courts to prosecute. I'd think either institution would regard private interference as dangerous and unnecessary. And I think they'd be right."

Jane thought Mel might be the author of that part of the script. "Did you tell them everything you knew, then?"

"Naturally. It was my duty. But I knew very little."

"Then you didn't see or hear anything suspicious?" Shelley put in.

"Suspicious? How? Aside from the fact that the woman died?" At this he smiled a real smile.

He obviously thought they were acting like idiots, and for a moment Jane wondered if he might be right. "You realize that one of the people at the dinner surely killed her and almost killed the maid?" she asked.

Bob Neufield reached for a pack of cigarettes, offered it to them, and lit one. "That's probably true," he said through a puff of smoke.

He was being so sensible and remote that Jane could hardly stand it. This was like

153

talking to a robot — or a military man. "Doesn't that bother you?"

"Not unduly. I don't know why it should. I didn't know the woman. I wasn't the perpetrator, nor was I the victim. I was merely a bystander, and so, I presume, were you ladies. Murder is an intolerable act, and must be punished, but that's not my job. I'm sure the police have their forces well in hand. I've always operated on the principle that the best way to help a man do a hard job is to stay out of the way unless asked to assist. You ladies might consider that."

Jane asked, "Did you tell the police what she said about you?"

She regretted the impulse the moment the words were out of her mouth. His jaw was set and he paled. His tone was that of furious anger barely held in check. "Yes, I did. It would be irresponsible to thwart the authorities by withholding any information, however little pertinence it has to the case." He stood up and walked to the door. "Ladies, I'm sorry, but I have a great deal of work to do and can't ask you to stay longer."

They slunk out.

Once in the car, Shelley said, "The man's long suit isn't the social graces."

"It's not exactly ours, either," Jane said. "If he's innocent, we've insulted him uselessly; and if he's guilty, we've laid our heads on the block. Jeez, Shelley, we really botched that up. You know, he could start another world war with that stuff in his back room."

"There's something that went through my mind. . . ." Shelley said, closing her eyes and motioning for Jane to keep quiet while she tried to recapture it. "Yes! I remember. Did you see that old canvas bag thing on the table to your left?"

"I don't know. What was it?"

"It had scissors and ration packets and a little vial. A kit. It made me think of something I saw in my grandfather's attic when I helped my mother sort it out. I showed the canvas kit to Paul, and he said the soldiers in World War One carried some kind of antidote to the poison gas. And sure enough, there was a vial with a needle in it in my grandfather's kit. Paul said it was dangerous to keep around. It was something they injected in themselves to counteract the effects of the poison gas —"

"And you think it could be a poison?"

"Isn't it possible?" Shelley asked, starting the car.

"I'm wondering, too, if the stories you hear about spies having a cyanide pill on them might be true. Would that sort of thing turn up in a military collection?"

"I don't know. I think cyanide works instantly. At least, it always does in books. But it would at least be worth asking VanDyne about. The police probably had no reason to look around Neufield's house. They weren't pretending to be guests, like we were. God, we behaved badly, Jane. Stupidly."

"Did you see that picture on the bookshelf?" Jane asked. "It was about the only photograph in the house. A pretty young woman."

"So?"

"So, I don't know. I just wondered if it was relevant."

Even Shelley's driving was subdued, a first in Jane's memory. As Jane got out, Shelley said, "Here. You forgot your book."

Jane looked at the copy of Mrs. Pryce's self-published diary that Shelley was handing her. "It's not mine."

"It must be. It's not mine. My copy is on the guest room desk. I put it there as I was leaving."

"I must have picked this one up with Katie's lunch sack without realizing it," Jane said. "See you at class tonight."

"Do you think we ought to go?" Shelley asked "What if he was the murderer and we just made him mad?"

"Shelley, it's not as if he doesn't know where to find us anytime he wants. We'll just turn down any homemade cookies he might bring and pass around."

They laughed uneasily and Jane went indoors. Her mother was sitting at the kitchen table, glancing through her copy of Mrs. Pryce's autobiography. Jane's copy was sitting on top of a cookbook next to the sink.

She looked down at the third copy in her hand.

— 13 —

Jane drove them to class that night in her ratty station wagon, having had all Shelley's driving that her nervous system could take for one day. "Shelley, this *must* be your copy of the book. It isn't ours," she said as they got into the car.

Shelley held up her own book in silent denial.

"I must have accidentally stolen someone else's," Jane said, perplexed. She stuffed the book into her purse.

They were the first to arrive at the city hall classroom, and Jane approached each of the class members as they came in. Bob Neufield was the first to arrive. She debated whether she ought to speak to him after their last run-in and almost kept quiet, but the extra book kept nagging her. Taking a deep breath for courage, she approached him. "Mr. Neufield, I think I may have inadvertently picked up something of yours," she said, holding out the book.

"I don't think so," he said, opening the briefcase he'd carried to class. There, in with the manuscript folders, was a copy of Mrs. Pryce's autobiography.

"Oh, it must be someone else's," Jane said. She took a deep breath and plunged in to an apology. "Mr. Neufield, I'm sorry if we offended you this afternoon. It certainly wasn't our intention."

He looked at her coldly. "No offense taken. I understand that ladies of your age with a lot of extra time on their hands sometimes get crazy notions."

Jane couldn't have been more insulted if he'd slapped her. She stared at him, trying to formulate a reply, and he looked back at her, smiling. This time it was a real smile, clearly victorious. Jane turned and went back to her seat.

"Jane, what's the matter?" Shelley asked. "Your face is crimson."

"I can't talk about it now," Jane muttered, her voice quavering with anger and embarrassment. Shelley and Cecily went back to discussing different kinds of apples, a subject that seemed to engage their entire interest at the moment.

Did the bastard think she was menopausal and that her hormones barely excused her? Did he picture her lounging around all day, eating bonbons and thinking of ways to waste a few more hours? On the

159

other hand, he might know perfectly well she didn't, but had gotten back at her in exactly the most vicious way possible. Mad as she was, she secretly thought she might deserve this comeuppance. After all, if he was as innocent as she, he had good cause to be offended at their questioning earlier.

Jane fumed silently for a few minutes and was starting to calm down a little when Ruth Rogers and Naomi Smith came into class. She approached them with the book. "No, it doesn't belong to either of us," Ruth said. "We found it so depressing that we threw our copies out. I didn't want to have anything like that in the house. Horrible woman. It's not nice to speak ill of the dead, but —"

Grady wouldn't claim it either. "Mine's in my car. I keep hoping I'll lose it, but I haven't gotten lucky yet. It was still in my car when I got here. Just pitch it, Jane. Nobody cares."

But Jane was starting to care and didn't know quite why.

"Missy, is this yours?" she asked when Missy came in.

"I hope not. The last thing I need is another one."

"No, I mean it. Did I pick it up from you somehow?"

160

Missy looked at her oddly, but looked in the canvas bag she carried her class materials in. She pulled out a copy. "This is the only one I carry around. The rest are still in the carton in my car. I'm going to set it out with the trash tonight. Are we all here? No, we're missing Desiree Loftus. Does anyone know if she's coming?"

Ruth raised her hand. "She called and asked me to tell you that she won't be here. She's not feeling well."

"Hung over," somebody muttered. Jane looked around but couldn't tell who'd said it.

"All right," Missy said, taking her place at the front of the room and commanding their attention. "We've had some upset here, so I want to briefly review some of the points we've already covered, then I'm going to go on to some observations and suggestions on chronology, flashbacks, flash forwards, and —"

Jane rummaged in the saddlebag purse for her notebook, still troubled by the mysterious extra copy of Mrs. Pryce's book. If it didn't belong to any of them, how did it get in Shelley's car? And why?

By the time class was over, she had pages of notes of ideas for organizing Priscilla's story. Listening to Missy's lesson, it occurred to her that it would be much more interesting if she started somewhere near the end of Priscilla's life, and suggested mysterious and dramatic things that had happened to her, then started back at the beginning.

A picture had formed in her mind of Priscilla as an old woman, dignified and aloof, living in near isolation in a house in the woods. And by her side, a wolf. A tame wolf, looking up at his mistress, ready to spring to her defense should an enemy come. She didn't know where the wolf idea had come from, but she liked it. If she started with this scene, with a lone horseman approaching — Priscilla calm, perhaps with a weary smile of welcome, the wolf alert, but looking to her to read her reaction to the visitor —

"Will you wake up!" Shelley said, nudging her as they came out of the building.

"Sorry, I was just thinking about —" Then she spotted why Shelley was prodding her back to the present tense. Mel VanDyne's little red MG was parked across the lot, and he was approaching.

"Later, Pris," Jane murmured as if she had to excuse herself to a real person. "Hi, Mel. I wasn't expecting to see you."

"I stopped by your house and realized you

must be here. How'd it go tonight?" His gaze swept the three of them.

"A very interesting class," Cecily answered.

"Nobody died," Shelley added.

Jane could see that Mel was surprised, maybe even offended, by Shelley's bluntness. He really didn't know anything about women, Jane realized. If they weren't fluffy, he didn't know what to make of them. He probably thought all mothers were really Donna Reed at heart.

"Glad to hear it," he said, turning to walk them to Jane's elderly station wagon. "Jane, are you free to go for a little ride? I could follow you home —"

"Go on, Jane. I'll drive your car," Shelley said.

"No, Mom can drive. I'm not insured for demolition derby drivers."

"Jane, I've *never* had an accident," Shelley reiterated.

"Why you haven't is one of the great mysteries of the universe," Jane said. "It ranks just behind 'Is there a God?' "

"Girls!" Cecily said. "Stop squabbling. I'll drive."

Mel grinned, and when he'd shown Jane to the car and got in himself, he said, "A mother is a mother forever."

"Dear God, I hope not!" Jane said, laughing. "It's a condition I hope to be eventually cured of."

"You don't mean that," Mel said, turning around and backing out. He put his arm across the back of the seats to do so. Jane liked the brief warmth of his arm against her shoulders.

"No, I don't. Mel, would you drive by Desiree Loftus's house? She wasn't at class."

"You think something's happened to her?" He was suddenly all business.

"No, I just want to be sure."

Mel found the house without being told the address. Jane realized that he must have a very retentive mind for details of an investigation. As they pulled up in front, however, Desiree could be seen in the front window, carrying a plant through the living room. "Want to go in?" Mel asked.

Jane was relieved. "No need. I was being an alarmist. Where are we off to?"

"I thought a Coke at McDonald's?"

"My kind of date," Jane said, then wondered if that had been the wrong thing to say. This wasn't exactly a date. It was more a casual pickup. She smiled at the thought of being picked up on the cusp of forty.

They got their drinks, then Mel drove to the mall, closed and deserted now, and

164

stopped and turned off the car in the middle of the huge parking expanse. "Just thought I'd fill you in a bit," he said.

Jane very nearly said, "Gee, I hoped we were going to make out," but thought better of it for several reasons, the primary being that it was too close to the truth. The other thing that stopped her was the realization that they probably didn't call it that anymore, and he'd feel as if he were out with his mother. Instead, she asked, "Any more word on the poison?"

"Not yet," he said. "I guess once you get past the usual things to test for, you've got a lot of weird stuff to work through. But I did find out a few things I thought might interest you."

"Yes?"

"Ah . . . Jane, you do realize this is highly irregular, don't you?"

"What is?" Sitting in a dark parking lot with a possible suspect? Taking an older woman out for a Coke?

"Talking to you about this case. I hope you'll keep anything that I tell you in strict confidence."

Jane considered seriously. "Except for Shelley. She's my Watson. Or maybe I'm hers. I haven't figured that out yet."

He didn't answer for a long moment.

"You don't like Shelley, do you?" she asked.

"It's not that —"

"She's very blunt. She not only says what she thinks, lots of times she says what *I* think and didn't know," Jane said. "I know you feel we're being terribly callous about all this, and we probably are, but women *are* tough, Mel."

He turned and smiled at her, condescendingly, she thought.

Maybe it was because she was still smarting under Bob Neufield's earlier insult, maybe she'd reached some turning point in her life, but she suddenly threw caution to the winds.

"Look here, Detective VanDyne, I know you're a big, macho cop. You think you've seen the real nitty-gritty of life, and housewives are just dust-bunny-brains worrying about trivialities, but you've got it wrong. Any woman who's had to turn a baby upside down and smack it nearly senseless to dislodge a penny stuck in its throat knows as much of life and death as you do — and in a much more personal way. We learn a lot about life, because mothers live it over again in each of their children. You've only gone through teenage angst once. I've been through it three times and still have one to go."

166

She was on a roll and couldn't seem to stop. "You think cleaning and cooking and vacuuming are stupid, but they're important. They make a safe haven. Those dumb, boring activities create a place where kids know they're loved, and no matter how badly life kicks them around, there's a place where somebody's doing her best to take care of them. You wouldn't be the person you are if it weren't for a caring mother. Men think they're so damned strong, but for God's sake, haven't you ever stopped to think who raised those strong men? Who taught them to be what they are? Women, that's who! 'Ordinary' women who clean up the cat shit and peel potatoes and make damned Halloween costumes and still manage to do the most important job in the world — raising the next generation!"

Jane stopped raving, shocked at herself.

She cleared her throat, took a reckless swig of her drink that nearly made her choke, and said, "Sorry. I must have suddenly been under the impression I was running for office."

Mel reached over, took the waxed cup from her hand, and dropped it out on the pavement. Then he put his hand on her cheek, leaned forward, and kissed her.

— 14 —

"So tell me everything that happened," Shelley said. "I want every intimate detail." It was nine o'clock Thursday morning, and they were having a cup of coffee in Jane's kitchen.

"Everything?" Jane said with a mock leer. "Not with my mother in the house."

"I heard that," Cecily said from the stairs. "Save the girlish confidences and tell me what he knows about Mrs. Pryce's murder," she added, coming into the kitchen and pouring herself a cup of coffee.

"Nothing on the poisoning," Jane said, setting out some sweet rolls she'd gotten at the bakery two hours earlier. "By the way, I'm supposed to swear both of you to secrecy. Actually, I'm not supposed to tell you at all, so you have to really, *truly* swear."

Her friend and her mother nodded solemnly.

"He was just telling me some of the stuff they'd found out about people in the class. Bob Neufield was kicked out of the army. He was given a . . ." She paused. "I've forgotten the word. It wasn't a dishonorable discharge, but it wasn't an honorable discharge either. Damn! How could I forget the term?"

"Never mind the word," Shelley said. "What was he thrown out for?"

"Couldn't tell. This whatever-it-is discharge means the army didn't bring any charges and it isn't a black mark against you. It just means the army no longer has any use for you. Mel says it's usually if the soldier has some habit or characteristic the army considers a liability — homosexuality, drinking, gambling, inability to get along with others. So there's no record of any charges because there weren't any. But they checked all his postings against General Pryce's, and there's no overlap whatsoever. Mrs. Pryce couldn't have met him before coming here."

"So why did she make that crack about him?" Cecily wondered aloud.

"The police are going on the theory that she was just raving. After all, it was nearly the last thing she said, and she was dying. They figure she was hallucinating and mixed him up with someone else. I can see that. He has a very anonymous military look even in civilian clothes. Imagine him in a uniform. He'd look like a hundred other

169

fair, fit, short-haired, middle-aged military men."

"You think they're right?" Cecily asked.

"I hope they are. We've pissed him off, and if he's a killer, that was real stupid," Shelley answered.

"What else?" Cecily asked.

"A lawyer turned up with Mrs. Pryce's will, which didn't have anything particularly interesting in it. It was a moderate estate, all the cash assets neatly put in trust for grandchildren. The maid, you'll be surprised to learn, gets the house and all that junk in it."

"She must have something on the old girl," Shelley said. "I can't imagine Pryce giving her a penny out of the goodness of her heart."

"She must have a lot on her," Jane said. "Mel says the maid's been with her since 1940. Just imagine fifty-some *years* with La Pryce. It's unthinkable!"

"What about the rest of the class?" Shelley asked.

Jane shrugged. "Nothing much we don't already know."

"Nothing!" Shelley said, outraged. "Can't the police do better than that?"

"They only know things about people if it's on an official record. Arrests, lawsuits, that kind of thing. And military records."

"Then we ought to turn crime investigation over to the IRS," Shelley said. She was still chafing over having been audited some months earlier. "They know everything. I imagine in some dusty file there's a record of what brand of toothpaste we all use."

"He did tell me that Grady once got a speeding ticket," Jane said. "To be fair, they probably could get more information if they knew exactly what they were looking for."

"Oh — so we're suddenly bending over backwards to be fair to the police," Shelley said. "Must have been some date."

"I was only out for an hour," Jane said.

"A lot of exciting things can happen in an hour," Shelley said.

Jane ignored her and turned to her mother. "Did you tell Katie I was out with Mel?"

Cecily nodded.

"What did she say? How did she react?"

Cecily sighed. "Just what you'd expect. She's a little jealous, a little embarrassed, a little understanding."

"I've been a widow for a year and a half," Jane said.

Cecily put up her hand. "Darling, you don't have to justify anything to me — or to Katie, for that matter. I think Detective VanDyne is a nice young man, and you de-

171

serve a life of your own. But you know we never think about our parents as real people. Think yourself back to that age. Imagine if your father hadn't been around and I'd have dated."

Jane drew back. "I'd have been appalled."

Shelley took a second sweet roll and buttered it. "It must be harder, too, for children whose parent has died. If it's divorce, they've undoubtedly seen a bit of the worst of both parents and can understand why they don't like each other, but Katie has no idea there was anything wrong between you and Steve —"

"She's not alone. Neither did I until he was packing to leave me for that bitch —"

"Don't get fired up. I just mean, she doesn't know that. She thinks that traffic accident was a sudden stop to a perfect marriage and took away a perfect daddy. She's bound to feel that you're betraying his memory."

"So what do I do about it?" Jane asked, instinctively turning back to her mother.

Cecily smiled. "Nothing. She'll adjust. Children are resilient, and so are mothers. Besides, at her age, her own life is much more interesting to her than yours."

"Sad but true," Shelley said with a laugh. "To get back to the subject at hand, what are we going to do? There are only two more classes, and I'm beginning to think that if we don't know anything by the end, we won't ever."

"I feel the same way," Jane said, "though I don't know why we should."

"So what's next?" Cecily asked.

"I thought maybe we could go visit Desiree. Just to see how she's doing and why she wasn't in class last night," Jane said.

"You think she couldn't face us without her guilt showing?" Shelley asked.

Jane wasn't sure if Shelley was serious or joking. "I've been reading Pryce's book this morning, and there's something I'd like to ask her about. Besides, I want to find out if that extra copy of the book is hers."

"Oh, Jane! Are you still going on about that?"

"Shelley, it's just a little weird thing that bothers me."

"Did you tell VanDyne about it?"

"Yes, and he considered it every bit as seriously as you do."

Shelley started clearing their plates. "I'd love to eat my words, but, Jane, there are a jillion copies of the damned thing floating around the class."

"Are you going with us, Mom?" Jane asked.

"No, I don't think so. Katie was stirring when I came down. I'll stick around and gossip with her. Why don't you leave the car, so we can buzz around if she wants."

Jane looked at her mother. "You are supposed to care deeply about my welfare. I delivered a little lecture on the subject last night. And yet, you're suggesting that I ride in a car with Atilla the Hun at the wheel."

"But she's never had an accident," Cecily said with a laugh.

"We were worried about you," Jane said to Desiree when she came to the door.

Desiree was holding a tissue to her red nose. Her eyes were red, too. "Sorry to miss it. Come in, girls."

Though it was summer, Desiree apparently had the furnace turned on. It was miserably hot in the house and smelled strange. "I'm cooking this cold," Desiree said before blowing her nose. "And I'm filling the air with medicinal herbs. In fact, I have a contractor coming over later to give me a bid on putting a greenhouse off the kitchen. Herbs are so important to our lives and so neglected. Herbs are the basis of all medicine, you know, and they can influence our mental, not to mention our psychic, state —"

174

Jane and Shelley exchanged "she's at it again" looks.

"I'm glad you girls came by. I wanted to talk to you about that field behind your houses —"

"It was supposed to have houses on it, but the builder went bankrupt. It's been tied up in court for years," Shelley said.

"And my cats will be crushed if anything ever is built there. That's their own private jungle," Jane added, feeling protective of the neglected field.

"But don't you see? It could be planted in wildflowers. It would be a lovely asset to the neighborhood, and people could have free access to the marvelous healing properties of the plants that would grow there."

"Not if it meant cutting through my yard, they couldn't," Shelley said.

Desiree wasn't the least put out at Shelley's practical turn of mind. She smiled sweetly. "But property is an illusion, my dear. We can't any of us own the earth. Not until we're buried and become at one with it."

"As long as I pay the taxes and the lawn service bills on it, I'm at one with it," Shelley said firmly.

Desiree was about to further her argument, but Jane was afraid this philosophical discussion could get out of hand. "Desiree, I've been reading Mrs. Pryce's book —"

"You have, my dear? Why ever would you do a thing like that? It's a terribly dangerous book."

"Dangerous? In what way?"

"It has a terrible black aura. But then, so did the woman herself."

Jane said, "I thought you said her aura was —"

"Jane!" Shelley cut her off.

"Yes, okay. I was saying, I noticed that Mrs. Pryce lived in Paris for a while in the early sixties. I thought I remembered you saying you did, too. Did you ever meet her there?"

Desiree looked taken aback. "Oh, I don't think so. I don't think she's the sort a person would forget, much as one would like to."

"But in my experience the American community in foreign countries is usually pretty clubby," Jane said. "Surely you would have run across her or heard of her."

Desiree laughed. "My dear, that's just what's wrong with Americans. They go off to fantastic places, then link arms and never see what's around them. In my travels, I always made a point of avoiding my coun-trymen."

Jane glanced at Shelley, who was shaking

her head in a "give it up" motion.

"Speaking of Mrs. Pryce's book," Jane persevered, "I seem to have an extra copy. I must have picked somebody else's up. Is it yours, do you think?"

"Oh, I have no idea, and frankly, I don't care where mine is." She paused, thinking. "However . . . if you've got an extra, I think I might use it as a weed killer in my yard." She glanced at the two of them and said, "Oh, I can see you scoffing, but psychic influence is very real, even if hard to capture in scientific terms. I once had a lovely oak tree in my yard that died, and I know it was because of the ugly patio furniture my sister-in-law gave me to set under it."

Shelley suddenly grabbed a tissue from the box on the coffee table and pretended to blow her nose. Jane could see her friend's shoulders shaking with laughter and was nearly infected herself. "Desiree, we won't keep you from your health routine," she said, fighting to keep control.

"Oh, do stay. I have some lovely snapdragon tea I just infused myself and some cornflower cakes."

Shelley snorted.

"No, really. I've got to run home and take Katie to work. We just wanted to see how you were. Thanks . . ." She hesitated, drawing a deep breath and pinching her own leg to cause some distracting pain. "Thanks, anyway. Shelley, come on! *Now!*"

They managed to get out of sight of the house before Shelley pulled over to the curb and put her head on the steering wheel, laughing helplessly. "Assassin lawn furniture!" she gasped. "I wonder if Stormin' Norman knows about it? He could have had K Mart ship a load to the Gulf and saved calling up all those reserves."

"Shelley, will you please get yourself together?" Jane said ten minutes later as they pulled into Shelley's driveway. They were both exhausted from laughter.

"All right. I'm over it," Shelley said, finishing this statement with a giggle.

"Now, this is serious. Listen to me, Shelley. The poison could have come from those plants she's got. And she denied having known Mrs. Pryce in Paris."

"Maybe because she didn't know her. It's possible, Jane," Shelley said, wiping her eyes. "As for the plants, I don't see how she could kill anybody with them, except by accident."

"Maybe it was."

"Come on, Jane. She just chopped up something, happened to carry a bottle of it around with her, and accidentally poured it on Mrs. Pryce's quiche at the exact moment nobody was looking? Not too likely."

Jane frowned. "You've got a point. Still, she can't really be as weird as she acts. Nobody could get through life that way. She might be really cunning and bright."

"Oh, I think she's smart. Some of the smartest people I know are the weirdest," Shelley said.

Jane arched an eyebrow. "You aren't referring to me, are you? Listen, Shelley, I know what I'm talking about on this Paris thing. I grew up all over the world, and believe me, even in a big city like Paris, the Americans who actually live there all know about each other, even if they've never met."

"But you're talking about normal people, Jane. Desiree is the type who would have lived in a commune, trying to teach the French to speak Esperanto or raise freshwater oysters or whatever her current interest happened to be. I can't see the diplomatic community throwing their arms wide and pressing her to their collective bosoms, can you?"

"Lord, no! Maybe you're right. But — although I hesitate to mention the subject — you notice she didn't produce proof that the extra copy of Pryce's book wasn't hers?"

Shelley put her hands to her head in exasperation. "So what? Jane, you're getting obsessed with this book thing."

"I don't know. I just think this book means something."

"It means you have sticky fingers and a dismal memory." Shelley leaned on the horn, and at Jane's questioning look, she explained, "Denise has an orthodontist's appointment in ten minutes."

Jane got out of the car just as Denise came flying out of the Nowacks' house and flung herself into the back of the minivan, saying, "Quick, Mom. Somebody might see me."

Her own house was quiet when Jane went inside. She looked in the garage. The car was gone, which probably meant that both her mother and daughter were away. She yelled up the steps to be sure. The only answer was blessed quiet except for the furtive jingle of Willard's tags as he came creeping out from his hiding place behind the sofa.

"Let's go outside, Lionheart," she said. She picked up the folder with her story about Priscilla and her copy of Mrs. Pryce's book and, grabbing a canned cold drink from the refrigerator, went out to the patio.

Just as she stepped outside, Meow came hurtling up over the back fence with a bird in his mouth. Jane quickly set down her things and took out after him, but he saw her coming and took the fence going the other way in a single bound without losing a feather. The bird was still in his mouth. Jane gave up. She felt honor-bound to save as many creatures as she could from the blood-thirsty cat, but drew the line at climbing fences and fighting her way through the field behind her house in order to do it. As her son Mike reminded her so often, nature was nature. But she remembered when he was a very little boy and got upset about the cats bringing in trophies. Now he had a squirrel tail collection on his bulletin board. The cats ate the squirrels they caught, but always left the tails for Mike.

She missed her son. Both her sons. She'd enjoyed the week of relative peace, but it was getting eerie. Life wasn't real without a jockstrap slung over the stair rail and ham-ster food ground into the carpet someplace. As much as she enjoyed seeing her children grow up, the thought of this house without them was horrifying. But she didn't need to worry about it now, she told herself. The boys were both due home tomorrow.

Tomorrow.

After tomorrow, she'd be back in the full mother routine. Driving everybody to friends' houses and lessons, arguing with Mike about how much of the time he could have the car, doing a million loads of laundry a day, and cooking madly, trying to keep their giant appetites satisfied. She'd lose most of her free time and probably any chance she had to figure out who'd killed Mrs. Pryce. And yet, she'd go on living in the neighborhood with the killer. She and her children. Without being able to guess what triggered the murder, they'd never be safe. The more she thought about it, the more fearful and angry she became.

She looked over her garden and was appalled at how many new weeds had grown in the few days she'd neglected the patch. She sat down, halfheartedly picking at some crabgrass that was encroaching on the tomatoes. She suddenly had the thought that people were like gardens: some of them productive or beautiful or both, others noxious and greedy. Mrs. Pryce was one of the weeds in life. And yet, the other plants weren't allowed to destroy the weeds. Only the Gardener could do that. She got up, depressed at the thought. She'd think about Priscilla instead. Or maybe Mel VanDyne.

She picked up her notebook and drink from the ground where she'd set them to chase Meow and started piling things on the patio table. That was when she noticed the little birdcage. It must have been part of Katie's shopping binge. She picked it up, smiling. It was a cute little ornamental cage made of fine bamboo, not large enough for a real bird, but a sweet little object to place on a shelf or fill with candies. Jane set it out of the way and took her legal pad out of the folder.

The thing she most wanted to do was put her feet up and think back over those few delightful minutes last night in the parking lot of the mall. Six, maybe seven, really expert kisses, before Mel had remembered that he was supposed to be working. Pity, that. But it had been wonderful to be in a man's arms again, even for such a short time. And it was great to be old enough to not care just where he'd learned to kiss so well. Age did have a few advantages.

She shook herself and said, "Get busy, Jane." She reread the last of what she'd written and had added another page of quickly scrawled work before she heard the car in the drive a few minutes later. It was probably Cecily and Katie returning. She put away her work and went back inside.

"Mom, I'm going to be late!" Katie shouted, flying through the kitchen.

Cecily was behind her, as placid and graceful as ever. "She didn't realize your car clock is slow, and I didn't know she needed to be at work at noon."

"It's okay. It's only three minutes away, and she's got four minutes. I'll take her. I've got to run to the store anyway," Jane said, taking the car keys and grabbing her purse. "That little cage is cute. I forgot to bring it in."

Cecily looked at her. "What cage?"

"The miniature birdcage. The little bamboo thing. Didn't you and Katie buy it?"

"Not that I know of." Cecily stood back as Katie bounced back past. She was now in her swimming suit and was hopping and pulling on her shorts over it as she went.

On the way to the pool Jane said, "Is that little birdcage on the patio table yours?"

"I don't have a bird. What would I want with a birdcage? Mom, can't you go faster? I'll be late."

Jane dropped her daughter, who walked across the parking lot as languidly as though she had hours to spare. Jane knew that was because Katie didn't want to jiggle. Jiggling wasn't cool in her crowd yet. Give them a few years.

Jane quickly consulted the list in her purse. She needed to get wine. She never drank it herself, but her mother was used to a glass with dinner, and she'd neglected this hostess duty so far. She also wanted to talk to Grady. She wasn't sure what she hoped to find out, but something interesting might slip.

Sadly, her visit to the liquor store put her in contact with one of the creeps who'd been asking her out ever since Steve died. She tried to avoid being noticed, but he spotted her and came oiling over where she was lurking behind the wine coolers. "Hey, Jane! Nice to see you. Lookin' good, honey. Lookin' good. Been gettin' any?" he said.

It was one of those moments Jane sincerely wished she were Katharine Hepburn. Kate would have known how to destroy this jerk with a look and a word or two. "Excuse me, Walt. I'm really in a frantic hurry."

She tried to edge past him, but he leaned against a precarious display of wine bottles and looked her up and down. "Come on, honey. Don't run away. I won't eat you — not unless you ask real nice. Ha, ha, ha."

Jane felt the red come up her neck. "If you say another word, I'm going to scream for the police."

"Aww, come on, don't be like that."

Jane drew a deep breath.

"Okay, okay, honey. Just joking," he said, stepping aside. By incredible good fortune, his foot dislodged one of the bottom bottles of the display, and Jane turned away to the sound of crashing and splashing.

As a clerk came running down the aisle, Jane said coolly, "I think that man is drunk."

She decided the wine could wait, especially since she didn't know where another liquor store was and certainly wasn't ever going back in this one. She backed out quickly and headed for Grady's office. It was twelve-fifteen. Maybe she could get him to go to lunch with her. But when she got to his office, she was told he always went home for lunch on Thursdays. "You just missed him, ma'am," the secretary said.

"I'll catch him there," Jane said. This suited her fine. More private. Possibly more revealing.

Grady's house was a small ranch style with a lush lawn and fresh paint. It was shaded by big elm trees that had somehow survived the blight, and all around the house were riots of flowers that grew in the shade. It was a very friendly, comfortable-looking house, like Grady himself. She rang the bell, mentally running over her excuse for calling while she waited.

The door opened a crack, and Grady's round, pink face appeared. "Ah, Jane . . ."

"Your office told me you were at home for lunch."

"Ah — yes. Well — would you like to come in?"

It wasn't a warm welcome, but she couldn't be choosy. "Thanks, Grady."

As he opened the door, she realized he was in a bathrobe. His legs and feet were bare. In the middle of the day? He noticed her look and said, "Spill. I spilled some paint on myself. Ran home to change clothes. Ah — sit down, won't you?"

He was a nervous wreck.

So much the better.

Jane sat down on the sofa by a picture window that had curtains pulled across it. "Grady, I just was wondering what you make of this whole thing with Mrs. Pryce. As mayor, I'm sure you're as concerned as I am that it be solved quickly and with as little publicity as possible."

"Ah — yes, of course." He was fumbling with a drawer in the end table. "Cigarette?" he said.

Jane wasn't sure whether it was an offer or a desperate plea. "Thanks, Grady, I have my own. Would you like one?"

She reached for her purse.

And picked up the wrong one.

Lying next to her purse on the sofa was a very distinctive moss green leather handbag.

Jane looked up and felt herself blushing for the second time in an hour. Grady was undressed in the middle of the day, and Missy's purse was on his sofa —

188

Jane stood up so suddenly that he stepped backward in alarm. "I left my cigarettes at home. I've got to go, Grady. Good-bye. No, don't see me out."

— 16 —

"In the middle of the day!" Jane exclaimed for the fifth time in as many minutes.

Shelley patted her shoulder and laughed. "Sit down. You'll get over it."

Jane threw herself into one of Shelley's kitchen chairs and fished around in her purse for the cigarette that provoked the revelation. "Missy and Grady. I can't believe it," she said, puffing furiously once she'd gotten the stale, battered object lighted. She'd been telling herself she was on the very brink of quitting for almost a year.

"Why not?" Shelley asked, sitting down across from her.

"Well, for one thing, she's a good six inches taller than he is."

Shelley laughed. "Jane, it doesn't matter when you're horizontal. Height is a purely vertical consideration."

"You know what I mean. It's the middle of the day that really gets me. They're grown-ups, not horny kids."

Shelley reached over and patted her hand.

"Jane, you really have been widowed too long. You're either obsessed with sex or appalled by it."

"I'm not appalled. Only hugely surprised. Grady and Missy! I had no idea!"

"Jane, people sometimes conduct perfectly happy affairs for years without anybody else knowing. Why do you think they should have let you in on it?"

"Years. My God! The secretary said he always goes home for lunch on Thursdays. Do you suppose . . . ?" She grinned. "Oh, I hope so. But in the daylight?"

"Didn't you ever make love in the daytime?"

"Oh, sure. But that was Steve," Jane said dismissively. "The stretch marks and wrinkles were his fault, so they didn't bother me. But an affair — an affair is different. I thought you had to have a gorgeous young body for an affair."

"There speaks the voice of inexperience," Shelley said. "Jane, get your mind out of Grady's bedroom and think about what this might mean. Do you think maybe Missy was upset on Grady's behalf about Mrs. Pryce's accusations? You told me Ruth was madder about the insult to her sister than Naomi herself was. What if it was like that with Missy and Grady?"

"Missy as a murderer? Impossible."

"But it's no more impossible to imagine than anybody else in the class."

"True. Except for Bob Neufield. He hates us, and probably with good cause. We should never have gone over there."

"Just like you shouldn't have gone to Grady's?" Shelley asked.

"Yes. It didn't stop me, did it? I've got to go home and stay out of trouble," she said, rising.

When she got in the house, the first thing she heard was the tapping of her typewriter. Cecily called from the living room, "I'll give this up if you want to use it."

"No. What are you doing?"

"I just remembered something that happened once that I wanted to jot down for my book. In spite of everything, I'm glad we took this class."

Jane almost told her mother that she was thinking about turning Priscilla's story into a book, but the idea was still too outrageous and fragile to share with anybody but Missy. Not that her mother would denigrate the idea, but there might be a fleeting moment of incredulity in her face, and Jane couldn't face it. "I'm going to work on my short story upstairs then," she said. "Remind me to tell you later what happened to the wine I was going to buy you for dinner."

An hour and several pages later, Jane came down to the kitchen to find a snack. The doorbell rang while she was trawling in the refrigerator. She opened the door. "Hi, Jane," Missy said. "Are we still speaking?"

"Oh, Missy, of course we are. Let's sit outside."

Missy threw the green purse down on the patio table and sank into a chair with a sigh. "I'm sorry I caused you to be embarrassed."

"Oh, no, Missy. It was my fault, not yours. I had no business at Grady's." Jane picked up the little bamboo birdcage and set it inside the back door, partly because she couldn't quite meet Missy's eyes yet.

"Poor Grady," Missy said with a smile. "He's such a dear conservative prude. You scared the daylights out of him, you know. I told him not to go to the door, but he's so super-responsible. It drives him nearly crazy when I let a phone ring without answering it."

Jane sat down across from her. "Missy — why Grady, if you don't mind my asking?"

Missy smiled. "Because he's a delightful pink teddy bear of a man. More important, I'm a big, homely woman, and he adores me."

193

"Of course he does!" Jane said sincerely. "How could he not?"

"I imagine you've told Shelley."

" 'Fraid so. I was so stunned. Why haven't you gotten married? Oh, I forgot. You've got a husband."

"Not anymore. He finally found someone else and divorced me about six months ago. No, the problem is Grady's wife."

"Grady has a wife? I didn't know that. Where is she? I've never met her."

"You don't hang around nursing homes. They were in a car accident the first year they were married. She suffered enormous brain damage. She's been in a coma ever since."

"I had no idea."

"No, and I hope you won't blab it. For all his outgoing personality, Grady's a terribly private person. He can't afford to divorce her. The bulk of her bills are paid by some insurance policy that would be canceled if they weren't married. It would take virtually every penny he makes to care for her. I've told him many times we could live on my money, but he's an old-fashioned frump who won't hear of it. That's part of the reason he's so careful about our relationship. The insurance company would, needless to say, love to unload him. He's afraid if we lived together or even made our arrangement official or public, they'd claim common-law marriage, bigamy, anything to cut off the benefits."

"They couldn't do that, could they?"

"They've already tried a couple of other stunts almost as nasty. He's had to drag them to court twice already. So now you know."

"I'm sorry. I didn't mean to snoop — well, it's exactly what I meant to do, but I was just wondering if he had any connection to Mrs. Pryce."

Missy sighed. "Actually . . ."

She stopped and looked hard at Jane as if making an appraisal, then said, "His wife is her great-niece. Mrs. Pryce never made the connection; Wells is a common name, and none of the family had any more to do with Mrs. Pryce than they had to. And since the community doesn't know about his wife, he didn't bring it to her attention. And before you ask, yes, the police know. Grady told your detective everything. Well, everything except about me, that is."

Jane sat back for a long moment. "You'll be glad to hear that Mel didn't breathe a hint of this to me. Can I tell Shelley? She won't say anything to anyone else. She's very happy you and Grady have each other, by the way."

"Just so long as she understands not to talk to anyone else."

They were quiet for a long moment, then Jane said, "It isn't an important connection, is it? Mel told me the money all goes to the grandchildren. Grady wouldn't benefit."

"Not a red cent. Jane, Grady had nothing to do with this murder."

"I believe you." And it was true. At least, she believed that Missy believed in his innocence. Jane herself wanted to think about it a little more before she checked Grady off her private list of suspects. She'd already drawn a light mental pencil line through his name, and nothing would make her happier than to dismiss him entirely. Unfortunately, she'd already penciled off everybody but Bob Neufield, and she had the strong feeling that, much as she'd like to cast him as a villain, he wasn't one.

"Jane, if we've hashed this over enough, I'd like to know if you've been working more on Priscilla's story. That's what I really came over about."

Jane started to tell Missy about the wolf idea, but Missy stopped her. "Bit of advice, Jane: Don't talk about an idea until it's already written. You'll use up all your fire on the telling, and the writing will be boring when you get to it."

196

"Oh — yes, I see. You're probably right. Well, yes, as you can see, I'm still working on it. Missy, do you really think I might end up with a published book? It seems impossible."

Missy chose her words with care. "I think you might end up with a *publishable* book. Whether it will get published is another thing. See, Jane, successful writing is made up of forty-nine percent discipline, and forty-nine percent talent, and two percent dumb luck."

"I don't even think I've got the discipline or the talent I need, let alone the luck."

"But those can both be nurtured and practiced and developed. The luck can't be."

"Don't you think I might do better to write a romance?"

"Good heaven's, no! Everybody thinks a romance is the easiest thing in the world to do, and it's one of the hardest to do well. Besides — the romance business is difficult."

"Why?"

"Because most of the romance editors are very young, very New Yorky. They think that anything west of the Hudson River is wilderness and that the typical reader is some hillbilly congenital idiot who has to move her lips to read. Consequently they tend to hold the writer down to Dick-and-Jane level. I once had an editor insist I remove a reference to Charles Dickens. She said the readers wouldn't have heard of him and they'd think he was a character in the book they'd missed. I'm not sure *she* knew who he was."

Jane laughed. "It can't all be that bad."

"No, some of the editors are very good, but you don't always get lucky enough to work with them." Missy had cheered up considerably. "There are a few other things you should know, if you're thinking of getting into this business. There are things that people will say to you that crush you the first six times or so, until you realize they're standard."

"Like what?"

"Like people who say, 'What name do you write under?' the implication being that they've never heard of you. I always tell them I write as Stephen King. Some of them get the joke. Some are more direct. 'Oh, you're a writer? I've never heard of you.' Or friends who will come up out of the blue and say to you, very pleasantly, 'I've never read one of your books.' I can't imagine what they expect you to say to that. And these aren't even the ghouls, Jane. These are

people trying to be nice and just not realizing how insulting and nasty they're being.
But the worst, and most common, is this
one: 'You're a writer? I always meant to
write a book — if I just had the time.' I'm
always tempted to say, 'Yes, and I've always
meant to be a brain surgeon if I could just
find time to try the surgery.' "

"Missy — I don't mean to pry into your
business, but can you make money writing?"

"Yes, but you can't count on it. It's feast
or famine. The nice thing is, there's not
much cost. It's not like opening a shop
where you have to pay rent and purchase a
huge amount of stock and pay employees
and buy a delivery truck. All you really need
is a typewriter and paper and your imagina-
tion, although I'd strongly recommend a
word processor. You're thinking about this
seriously, aren't you?"

"Semiseriously," Jane admitted.

She got up, gave Jane a hug, and said,
"Most of the time I think writing is the best
job in the world. You get to stay home, wear
whatever you want, and smoke without anybody complaining. And I better get back to
work."

Jane walked to the car with her. As Missy
got in, she said, "Look at your front porch.
Flowers, I bet."

Sure enough, there was a large cone of white paper sitting on the porch.

Jane bid Missy good-bye and walked back to the house. She took the flowers in and tore off the paper. It was a lovely fresh arrangement, all in blues and whites in a glazed white bowl. Jane searched among the blooms for a card, but there was none. She noticed the name of the florist on the wrapping paper, but decided not to call and ask.

It must have come from Mel, she thought. What a nice, romantic gesture.

— *17* —

"What a beautiful arrangement!" Cecily said, looking at the flowers that were still sitting on the kitchen counter. "Who are they from?"

"I presume they're from Mel, but there's no card. What are all these things, anyway? I think this is a Shasta daisy, but I don't recognize any of the blue ones."

"I don't either. Jane, is this serious? With Mel?"

"Oh, Mom, I don't know. I don't think so. We don't have anything in common."

"Sometimes that doesn't matter," Cecily said. "In fact, that very thing can be a good basis for a relationship. It means constant discovery."

"Except Mel isn't interested in discovering my world — housework, kids, homework, school carnivals. And I can't say that I blame him. It's all necessary, but it's not fascinating. And frankly, I feel the same about his job. Necessary, but pretty boring except times like this when it has a connection with me. I can't see us ever having scintillating conversations about what kind of powder they use to pick up fingerprints."

"Jane, dear, you're talking about jobs, not what you are inside."

"But, Mom, I've been a housewife and mother for so long that what I *do* has become what I *am*."

The phone rang. "Hello? Oh, hi, Mel," Jane said.

Cecily found a sudden errand to do elsewhere.

"Mel, Missy told me about Grady."

"Oh? What did she tell you?" he asked cautiously.

"That his wife's been in a coma for ages and is a relative of Mrs. Pryce's. You hadn't mentioned that."

"He asked me to keep it confidential, and I agreed to if it had no bearing on the case."

"And it doesn't?"

"So far, it appears not. His wife isn't closely enough related to inherit. There are at least seven grandchildren ahead of her. And even if they were gone, there are a couple great-grandchildren. We've also had accountants going over the city's books. Unless Grady's twice as smart as all of them put together, there isn't a penny missing. How come Missy told you this? How did she know?"

"Oh, they're friends, I guess. It probably

202

had to do with his autobiography for class," Jane said. If Mel could keep a confidence, so could she.

"We have a policewoman skimming her books, too."

"Why?"

"To see if there's any suggestion in any of them that she's knowledgeable about poisons."

Jane laughed. "Mel, they're romances. People don't get poisoned in romances. And frankly — no, never mind." She'd been about to lambaste him for having a police*woman* read the books, as if the books weren't something a man could bother with. Or maybe a man would have his machismo impaired by close association with romances. But she wasn't sure he was ready for another lecture or that she wanted to risk giving one.

"You never know," he said mildly, not realizing what he'd missed.

"Mel, thank you for the flowers. They're absolutely beautiful. I'm going to keep them here in the kitchen where I can enjoy them while I work."

There was a long silence on the other end of the line. "Flowers? Somebody sent you flowers?"

"It wasn't you?"

"No, I'm afraid it wasn't."

"Oh, how embarrassing. I'm sorry. But if it wasn't you —" She stopped, realizing it wasn't a good idea to mention that there was no one else in the world who would think to send her flowers. "There wasn't a card, and I thought —"

"No," he said tightly. "It must have been another admirer."

"Maybe so," she said with hysterical brightness. "So, is there anything new with the investigation?"

He was silent for a minute. Then, "No, we're plodding along. Don't worry, though. We'll get the crucial evidence eventually. If a killing isn't a clear domestic disturbance, which most of them are, it usually takes some time to work it out step by step. You have to understand, Jane, that with all the technical advances in law enforcement —"

Jane wasn't listening to his lecture. She was staring across the room at the flowers. If Mel didn't send them, who the hell did?

She waited until he'd wound down and said, "Oh, I almost forgot. Desiree Loftus is on an herb binge. Shelley and I went over there, and her house is full of plants. She's brewing up health teas and things."

She didn't need to explain to him why it might be important. "Okay, we'll check it out." He held his hand partially over the phone and had a muffled conversation, then came back to her and said, "Sorry, I've got to go."

"I'll talk to you later. Good-bye," Jane said.

Nice. He either forgot the purpose of his call or there was no purpose except to talk to her.

Jane stood for a moment, then called Missy's number. She got her answering machine. She hated talking to the things, but in this case, did. "Missy, this is a stupid question, but would you call and confirm that Grady didn't send me those flowers that were on my front porch? I know he didn't, but I need to be sure —" There was a click as the answering machine hung up. Missy apparently didn't like getting long messages and had it set accordingly.

Cecily came in the kitchen door from the backyard. "Do you have some gardening gloves? Your vegetables are getting overgrown with weeds."

"I've even got an extra pair," Jane said. "Mom, Mel didn't send those flowers."

"How exciting. You must have a secret admirer."

She and her mother spent an hour in the yard, weeding and talking. This time Jane had no great theological insights, just a nice

205

visit with her mom. Jane told her about the visit with Desiree and also about her embarrassing intrusion into Grady's life. She knew her mother wouldn't have any cause to speak to anyone about Grady and Missy, but swore her to secrecy in any case. "Oh, I forget. Your wine." Jane recounted her horrible visit to the liquor store.

"The dreadful man! How nice to see justice done once in a while. He didn't get hurt, did he?"

"I don't think so. He was still bellowing about how it was all somebody else's fault when I left."

"Jane — maybe he's your secret admirer."

"Oh, I hope not! No, he couldn't be. A man who asks a woman if she's 'getting any' wouldn't have the grace and romance to send flowers. He'd be more likely to send a vibrator — or one of those cakes from an obscene bakery. No, I think it's probably Grady. He knew I was as embarrassed as he was. They're probably apology flowers. I put in a call to Missy to find out, but I got her machine."

"I imagine you're right. Jane, tell me about this story you keep going back to working on."

Jane sat back and brushed dirt off her gloves. "I'm almost afraid to talk about it.

Missy says it could be a book."

"How wonderful." There wasn't a scintilla of disbelief in her voice. Just genuine pleasure.

"No, it's really not. I don't know the first thing about writing a book, and I feel like a fraud even saying it."

"Nobody knows if they can write a book until they try it. I think you should give it your best shot. If it doesn't pan out, you'd have had a good time trying. Tell me about it. It's a novel, right?"

"I can only tell you about the part that's written. Missy says so."

"Then tell me that."

Cecily had some interesting ideas for plot twists, and she enthusiastically supported Jane's idea of using part of her inheritance from her friend to buy a computer. "You're in the Stone Age nowadays if you don't have one. You could also do your household bookkeeping on it and get some games for the children. On second thought, that part's probably counterproductive," Cecily said. When they finally went back into the house, Jane was bubbling with ideas and had, in addition, four little cucumbers that had actually grown on her side of the fence to make into a salad. "Jane, I'll make dinner. You work on your book," Cecily said.

"I can't do that. You're a guest."

"Yes, you can. I'm your mother and I'm telling you to go write. Give me the car keys. I've got a new recipe I want to try out on you."

Jane spent the rest of the afternoon blissfully involved with Priscilla. She made one quick run to the library to get a book on Colonial costume and another on social customs, but didn't let herself get sidetracked into reading them yet.

Nor did she consciously let herself think about Mrs. Pryce's murder. But it kept running through her mind like a dark undercurrent. Missy, Grady, Bob Neufield, Desiree, Ruth, Naomi, and Maria Espinoza kept popping into her thoughts, and she kept shoving them aside.

And other thoughts kept crowding in at her, too. The extra book in Shelley's car, the little birdcage, the beautiful flower arrangement. Were they, in some obscure way, threats? Somebody was giving her things. Of course, the book and birdcage could have been accidental. Things that just got left someplace and had nothing to do with her. But the flowers — what about the flowers? They weren't accidental. Someone deliberately sent her flowers. They went in and ordered and paid for them.

"Jane! Dinner's ready!" Cecily called up the stairs. Jane glanced at her watch and was astonished to see that it was already six o'clock. Where had the time gone?

"Mom, that was great," Jane said, taking one last bite of cucumber. Cecily had fixed a chicken casserole dish with peas and water chestnuts that was layered with lasagna noodles and white sauce and cheese-crusty on the top.

"It's the curry powder."

"I didn't taste curry." Jane started clearing the table.

"That's the secret. There's not a chicken dish in the world that can't benefit from a breath of curry. Jane, I'll do that. You've got to get to class."

"Me? Aren't you coming?"

"Not tonight. Katie called while you were in the basement throwing things in the dryer. She said there's some problem with the chlorine tanks and they're closing the pool tonight at seven. She wanted to know if we could go to a movie. I told her you needed to go to class, but that I'd like to go. You can take notes for me, can't you?"

"I'd be glad to. Are you sure you don't mind missing it?"

"I'd feel a lot worse about missing a

chance to go out with my granddaughter. You better catch Shelley, though. I'll need your car."

Jane dialed Shelley and made the arrangements. On the way to class a few minutes later, Jane told about the flowers she'd received. "They aren't from Mel. I don't think they're from Grady, but I never heard back from Missy. I'm sure they didn't come from the slimeball —"

"What slimeball in particular?"

"Oh, didn't I tell you about the liquor store? You'll love this —"

The story took them all the way to the parking lot of the city hall. They were sitting in the car laughing when Missy pulled in. She came over to Shelley's car. "Jane, sorry I couldn't return your call. I did check with Grady. He said no, he didn't send them, which isn't surprising. Grady doesn't 'do' flowers. I send myself a poinsettia every Christmas in his name, and also a nice corsage of gardenias for my birthday. He always pays the bill, but never thinks of taking on the whole job himself. Where's your mother, Jane?"

Jane explained.

"There are Ruth and Naomi. Grady's picking up Bob because his car wouldn't start. They ought to be along in a minute.

I'm going in and get my notes in order."

"We'll come in in a sec," Jane said. When Missy had left, Jane turned to Shelley. "If Grady didn't send me the flowers, who did? And, Shelley, I haven't even told you about the birdcage yet."

"Birdcage? Jane, is Mel picking you up?"

"I don't think so. He called this afternoon, but he didn't say anything."

Shelley tapped her nails on the steering wheel thoughtfully. "You haven't filled me in on your date yet, either. Jane, we need a serious talk. This has gone on long enough! We've got to get everything sorted out and someone arrested."

— *18* —

Jane hadn't really expected Mel to be waiting for her to get out of class again, but that hadn't kept her from hoping — and from being disappointed when he wasn't there. She and Shelley went back to Jane's house and found that Cecily and Katie weren't home from the movies yet. "All right," Shelley said, all business, "show me this birdcage."

Jane had to think a minute before she remembered that she'd set it inside the garage door. She brought it in and set it on the kitchen table. Both women sat down and stared at it for a moment. "It's not a real birdcage," Shelley said. "I've seen this before."

"Have you?" Jane looked at it, and her eyes widened in recognition. "Yes, so have I, come to think of it. It had candies in it when I first saw it. That's what I first thought of when I found it. But where —"

"Put it at the back of your mind. It's easier to remember things that way. So, where did you find it?"

"On the patio table."

"When?"

"This morning. After we got back from Desiree's house. I went outside and it was on the patio table."

"How long had it been there?"

"How would I know, Shelley? It didn't come with a timer."

"I mean, when was the last time it *wasn't* there?"

It only took Jane a few seconds to interpret this question. "I can't remember if I went out there earlier today. Wait. Yes, I got up very early and had a cup of coffee outside."

"And it wasn't there then?"

"I'm not sure. It was awfully early, and Willard was out there with me, threatening to go into bark mode and wake up the neighborhood. I was keeping a close eye on him. As close an eye as I can muster early in the morning. I couldn't swear to it, but I don't think it was on the table then."

"So all we know for sure is that it wasn't there *yesterday* morning."

"Yesterday? Oh, yes. You and Missy and I sat out there."

"And were you out again yesterday or last night?"

"I don't think so. I let Willard and the cats

in and out about a hundred times, but you can't see the table from the kitchen door that goes out back."

"The Purple Porcupine!" Shelley said suddenly.

"What?"

"That little gift shop at the mall. That's where I've seen it."

"You're right. Last week when we were looking for something for Denise's birthday. There were about a million of them," she added sourly.

"And they've had them for months," Shelley added. "Anybody could have had one. I'm not so sure it means anything anyway."

"Neither am I," Jane admitted. "But taken with the extra copy of the book and the flowers, it's odd."

"I still think you're wrong about the book being a mystery. You just accidentally picked up somebody else's. And the flowers; are those the ones?"

Jane carefully picked up the arrangement from the counter and set it in the middle of the table. "Pretty, isn't it?"

"Gorgeous. Set somebody back a pretty penny. Why don't you call the florist and ask if they have a record of who sent it?"

"I thought about it, but got interested in

Priscilla and forgot to do it."

"Priscilla? Who's that?"

Jane took a deep breath and explained to Shelley about the concept of writing a book.

"Jane! That's the job answer, don't you see? If you're any good at it, you can do it in your own time, make some extra money. This is a great idea. What's the name of the book?"

Murder was forgotten for the moment.

"I don't know. There's a wolf in it, and I'd like to work 'wolf' into the title. It's a dark story, sort of gothic, and 'wolf' is a great word for that mood. But it can't just be *Wolf* for a title. It would sound like a publication of the National Geographic Society."

"Hmmm. Wolf whistle. Wolf in sheep's clothing. No. All wrong. Wolf pack —"

"No. Cry wolf?"

"Maybe. Depends on the story. Holding a wolf by the ears —"

"What's that mean?"

"It's Greek, I think. It's the same as holding a tiger by the tail. Gone to the wolves?"

"That's dogs. Gone to the dogs."

"Oh, yeah. She-wolf? Wolf bane? Wolf at the door?"

"Wolf bane . . ." Jane mused. "I like that. Bane is a good word. Gothic, a little spooky and ominous. A hint of the psychic. What is wolf bane?"

"I have no idea. A plant, maybe? Or a drink? It couldn't be a place, could it?"

"No, I think it's a plant. I'll look it up. I like the sound of that. I hope it's appropriate and isn't a disfiguring disease or something."

"Good. We've solved one of the really important questions in life," Shelley said wryly. "Now all that's left is murder. Frankly, I don't think the birdcage and flowers have anything to do with it."

"You're forgetting the extra copy of Mrs. Pryce's book."

"I was trying to."

"But why would anybody leave the birdcage on the patio?"

"How about this: Somebody saw it, thought you'd like it, and came over to give it to you. Maybe, when they saw your car wasn't here, they sat down on the patio to wait and see if you came home soon. When you didn't, they left it for you."

"Without a note?"

"Didn't have a pen and paper along. She meant to ask you later if you got it and hasn't run into you yet."

"But everybody was in class but my mother."

"I don't mean anybody in class, Jane. Just some friend. Your uncle Jim — well, maybe not — or Suzie Williams. Maybe it was for Katie!"

"Katie doesn't have admirers who could afford a flower arrangement that cost a good sixty bucks."

"No, but that's a different matter."

"Is it? I still think there's a connection."

Shelley sighed. "All right. Let's suppose there is — only for a moment, mind you. I don't want to encourage these delusions. What would a book, a toy birdcage, and flowers have to do with the murder, and much more important, if they do have to do with it, why would someone give them to you?"

"As hints? Clues?"

"But who would do that? The murderer? If he wanted to get caught, he'd just tell the police without you. And if he didn't, he wouldn't mess with you either."

"For the thrill of it? To increase the danger?" Jane said, but shook her head as she was speaking. "What if somebody else knows or thinks they know who did it?"

"Same questions," Shelley said. "Why tell you instead of the police, and why not say it right out if they wanted the person caught? Likewise, if they wanted to protect the murderer, they'd protect him instead of strewing clues around on purpose."

Jane leaned back in her chair and stared past Shelley at Meow swishing his tail furiously, pretending there was a mouse under the stove. At least Jane hoped he was pretending. "All right. I give up. You must be right. But it is still strange, especially the flowers."

"I'll grant you that. But strange and murderous aren't synonyms. There's probably a boring, logical explanation for the flowers. Like the florist just delivered them to the wrong house by mistake. Now, we're going about this backwards. We need to consider the people as suspects, one by one. Go over everything we know about them and see if we can't at least eliminate a few."

"I have a lot of information about Grady that I haven't told you yet. Missy said I could, but only if you swore it would go no farther."

Shelley dutifully swore, and Jane told her about Grady's wife and her relationship to Mrs. Pryce. She also added what Mel had said about Grady's wife being so far down the list of heirs that there was virtually no motive at all.

"Still," Shelley said slowly. "It might not be about money. It probably isn't, in fact.

She didn't have that much, and nobody had any reason to suppose she had secret fantastic wealth." As Shelley was talking, she got up and went to Jane's refrigerator to pour herself some orange juice. Jane gestured, and Shelley fixed her one, too. "Jane, what if they'd had some terrible family blowup? Just imagine that she was responsible, in some peripheral way, for Grady's wife's accident. Might he not hate her enough for how she's wrecked up his life to kill her?"

It was Jane's turn to throw cold water on a theory. "Why wait till now? The wife's been in a coma for years, probably decades, if they married young."

"Maybe he just never got the chance before."

Jane looked at her skeptically.

"Grady's got to be an awfully patient man," Shelley said.

"And a pretty stupid one if he couldn't think up a way to bump her off without waiting years to be invited to dinner with a mob of other people."

"Maybe you're right. All right, let's go through everybody then. Grady Wells —"

"Motive," Jane said, "possible revenge for —"

"No, get a piece of paper. First, what we

know, then the possibilities."

Jane fetched a notepad and pencil — and let the cats in while she was up. She headed the page SUSPECTS. "Okay, what we know Grady could have had against her is that she was accusing him of embezzling city funds."

"And put under that, 'Not likely to be true,' " Shelley instructed her. "Then on the other side of the page, the possible theories like a family row involving his wife."

Jane did as she was told, and they both sat and looked at the page for a while. "I'd give him a seven out of ten," Jane said. "For a real motive and a possible one." She wrote a 7 next to his name.

"Missy," Shelley said. "Real motive: Pryce accused her of writing pornography."

"Theoretical motive: to protect Grady," Jane said. "Another seven?"

"No! Missy's so nice, I'd feel like a traitor giving her a seven."

Jane looked at her and spoke sternly. "This has nothing to do with liking people. We like everybody but Bob Neufield. This is a purely intellectual evaluation."

"All right. A seven."

"Maybe even an eight for both of them," Jane said. "Just on the grounds that they're both so damned good at keeping a secret.

220

Not that having an affair is really under-handed, but the way they've kept it quiet does show a certain cunning."

"Seven and a half," Shelley said.

"Desiree Loftus."

Shelley considered. "Pryce called her a drunk. If she is an alcoholic and knows it, that might have really gotten to her. And there's the means, too. All those herbs."

"Both pretty thin," Jane said. "I wouldn't give her over a three."

"You're forgetting the Paris connection that you were so het up about earlier."

"Oh, yes! Well, maybe with all three, a six? What about Bob Neufield?"

"A ten!"

"No, Shelley, intellectual consideration, remember?"

"Pryce accused him — we think — of ho-mosexuality. To a military man, that would be a motive. Especially if it wasn't true."

"But she was raving. And Mel says his military discharge doesn't bear it out."

"That's what I mean. If he was discharged for some other reason entirely, he couldn't fight the slander with the truth, because it would be embarrassing, too."

"But she didn't even say it outright, like she did with Grady and the embezzling ac-cusation. Shelley, I don't think we can give him more than a two."

"A two! With an arsenal in his back room?"

"She was poisoned, not blown up. I'll give him a three, if it will make you happy. Now, who else? Ruth and Naomi."

"One at a time. Naomi: Pryce was rude to her about her illness."

They looked at each other, trying to think of anything else. "She collects cookbooks," Shelley added.

"Cookbooks tell you how to feed people, not how to poison them," Jane pointed out.

"Okay. Right. What if the blood disease she has is AIDS and she doesn't want anyone to know? You know how weird people are about AIDS. She could be a lot more sensitive to that sort of 'get away, you're contagious' talk than she let on. Don't look at me like that. I'm just theorizing."

"Two, tops," Jane said, writing the number down.

"Then Neufield has to be more than a three."

"What about Ruth?"

"No motive except secondhand on her sister's behalf. A one at the most."

"Don't be hasty. She's a very strong-minded woman. Takes action when it's called for."

"So do we, and it doesn't mean we're murderers."

"Who's left? The maid."

Jane put her pencil down. "She's a real unknown, isn't she? She could have tons of motives we'd never guess. Do you think maybe that's why they're keeping her in the hospital so long? A sort of subtle house arrest?"

"What's VanDyne told you about her?"

"Not much. And for all his apparent openness, he can keep confidences. He knew all about Grady's wife and didn't say anything about her. He might know all kinds of things about the maid."

"I think we have to give her a ten with a question mark."

Jane looked at the list again. "Well, on the theory that it's the least likely person, it has to be Ruth or Naomi."

"Or you, me, or your mother. We're all zeros," Shelley pointed out. "Not even on the list, in fact.'

"Good point."

Headlights swept the room as Jane's station wagon turned in to the driveway. Shelley glanced at her watch. "My God! Paul will think I've been kidnapped." She hopped up and headed for the door, setting the empty juice glasses in the sink as she went. Jane stuffed her notes in the kitchen junk drawer.

Shelley opened the door and turned back. "Jane, you didn't tell me a thing about your date with VanDyne."

Jane grinned. "I didn't, did I?"

— 19 —

Jane stayed up late that night talking with her mother and daughter. Not about the murder, but about practically everything else. At one point, Cecily asked Katie point-blank, "What do you think about your mother dating?"

That led to another hour of talk, some tears, a few feeble jokes, and a final understanding that Jane Jeffry wasn't entirely over the hill, and might as well go out with men occasionally — so long as those men knew that Steve Jeffry had been a saint.

Jane repressed the urge to remind Katie how she'd felt about her dad when he'd forbidden her to wear lipstick, or to go to the mall with her girlfriends. Shortly before his death, they'd nearly come to blows over whether she could wear jeans with the knees deliberately torn out. But then, maybe Katie would eventually forget about her tiffs with me as well, Jane told herself.

"I'm glad you got that out in the open, Mom," Jane said to Cecily as they climbed the stairs shortly before one o'clock.

"There's a lot you learn as a mother," Cecily said, yawning. "And there's a few things you don't understand until you're a grandmother. Like the benefits of just wading in and thrashing it out. I wish I'd done that when you were at home."

"It's too late now," Jane said with a smile.

"And not necessary anymore, I hope."

"I'm glad you waded right in."

Cecily stopped midstep and took a deep breath. "Darling, I've learned something about myself lately. I'm a better grandmother than I was a mother."

"You were a wonderful mother. You still are."

"No. You're a much better mother than I was. You're always here for the children. I wasn't. I'm proud of you. I guess I should have said that a lot sooner. Good night, chickie."

Jane hugged her, her eyes brimming with tears. "You haven't called me chickie in ages. I kinda like it."

Jane couldn't get to sleep for an hour. In a couple sentences, her mother had wiped out years of hidden resentments. Somehow, the fact that Cecily knew she'd failed, if only in a very small way, eliminated Jane's grudge about it. It shouldn't have been that simple, but it was. Maybe all she'd been waiting for was an apology. Now she found herself wondering whatever had given her the idea that her mother *had* to be perfect? Yes, Jane and her sister had missed a few things, but they'd had so many wonderful benefits that other children missed. And if her mother had been a little too devoted to her husband, why, maybe that was Jane's problem of perception. If she'd loved Steve as much as her mother loved her father, Jane would still have a husband. Maybe her own less than perfect marriage had colored her views with a little jealousy.

Her mind kept going over the talk with Katie, too, thinking of a dozen things she could have said better, and finally she came back, inevitably, to her earlier conversation with Shelley about Mrs. Pryce's death. She went back over that discussion, too, with no more result than the first time. The artificial deadline she'd formed in her own mind was looming before her. Tomorrow night would be the last class. She wanted desperately to figure it out by then, before everybody scattered and went on to other interests. No doubt Mel was right — patient police work would provide the solution sooner or later. It was the "later" that worried Jane. The more time passed, the more chance there was of someone else coming to harm.

She finally fell asleep and had nightmares. A long line of trucks was driving up and delivering flowers. Masses of flowers, suffocating tons of flowers. They covered the windows like a colorful avalanche. The weight was making the windowpanes break, and flowers were cascading in. Jane kept trying to sweep them up, but couldn't. The scent of them started to choke her. She tried to hide the children in the little birdcage, certain for some reason that they'd be safe in there.

She woke up at nine, sweating and distressed. The cats were sitting on the end of the bed, looking at her. Willard was on the floor beside her, snoring. She showered quickly, then checked on her mother and Katie. Both were still sound asleep. Pulling on culottes and one of Mike's T-shirts that had gotten mixed up with her laundry, she went downstairs with the cats wreathing their way between her feet and meowing piteously. She fed them and Willard and started the coffee maker.

Somehow, these repellent domestic chores were comforting. She wondered if men felt the same way about mowing the lawn. Fat chance. Thinking of men made her think of Mel. And that made her think about what she looked like. What if he dropped by and she looked as if she'd been left out in the rain all night?

She ran a comb through her hair, fluffed it up a little — no point in going the whole hot roller route — and put on makeup. She glanced in the mirror when she was through. Not terrific, but not downright scary, either.

Still no sounds from upstairs. She rummaged in the junk drawer and pulled out her notes that she'd made the night before with Shelley. She went back, suspect by suspect, but had no new insights. At the bottom of the last page, she'd doodled the words "wolf bane." She'd meant to look it up, but more pressing matters had intervened.

She put away the notes, took down the dictionary from where it sat next to the cookbooks, and hunted. It took her a while to discover it was "wolfsbane." But the dictionary wasn't much help, except to say it was a plant and give its botanical name. Well, at least it *was* a plant, she thought, not a disease or a hairstyle or something equally useless.

Putting the dictionary back, she took down a fat, battered garden encyclopedia she'd found at a garage sale a couple months earlier. Under Wolfsbane she found, "A popular name for *Aconitum lycoctonum*. See Monkshood."

She put the heavy book down on the counter, bending a few pages at the corners as she turned back to the M section. A bell was tinkling at the back of her mind, and she suddenly felt rushed. There . . . "Monkshood — a common name for genus *Aconituin,* tall perennial herbs grown for showy blue flower spikes. All parts of plant are highly poisonous. Not to be grown near vegetables or in a garden where children might play. See Plate 17."

Jane found Plate 17 and looked at it for a very long time. She held her breath as she turned slowly and looked at the flower arrangement on the kitchen table. She took the book over, set it down next to the arrangement, and studied them both again.

"My God," she whispered.

Picking up the flower arrangement as if it could go off like a bomb any second, she carried it to the guest bathroom off the kitchen, set it on the floor, and closed and locked the door. She sat back down at the kitchen table, her mind racing erratically.

Aconite.

She remembered the name vaguely from her days of working in Steve's family pharmacy. Locked up. Warning labels. Could be handled only by the chief pharmacist. Old-fashioned skull-and-crossbones label.

Jane reached for the phone book, looked up the number of the florist shop. She thought nobody was going to answer, then on the seventh ring, a whiny teenaged boy answered. She could practically hear the pimples. Jane gave her name and address. "I need to know about the flowers you delivered here yesterday."

"Why? Was there something wrong with them, lady?"

"No. Just look up the delivery record. Please. It's very important."

"Okay," the boy said in surly voice. "What's the address again?"

She told him, then waited a terribly long time. He finally came back. "Naw, lady, we didn't bring nothing to you yesterday."

"What about the addresses on either side of me? Maybe it came to the wrong house?"

"Naw, nothing there either," he said after another interminable wait.

"Are you positive about this?"

"Sure, lady. Whatsamatter?"

"Nothing. Thank you."

It was the answer she expected — and feared.

She could hear a shower running upstairs. *Think, Jane. You've almost got it.* She paced back and forth, pieces falling into place in her mind with sickening thuds. She searched frantically for a copy of Mrs. Pryce's autobiography. *One day the house is littered with the damned books, and when you need it, there s not one anyplace,* she fumed to herself. She finally found her mother's copy and thumbed through. She found the page she was looking for and read it over twice, then dog-eared the corner and closed the book.

Yes, it all fit. The flowers, the birdcage, the book. She'd been right. Her instinct had told her they were important, and now she knew why. And it seemed so obvious now that she couldn't imagine why she hadn't seen it immediately.

But why? Why?

She went down to her office in the basement, where she could phone without being disturbed or overheard. She dialed the police station. "Is Mel VanDyne in, please? It's important."

"He was here a while ago. Think he left. I'll see. Hold on."

She could hear the clack of typewriters and the murmur of voices. There was a high-pitched laugh closer to the phone. "Come on, Mel. Be there," she said to herself. Her heart was beating at twice the rate it should be, and she felt breathless from running *down* the stairs.

"Yes?"

"Mel. It's Jane. Thank goodness I caught you."

"Jane, what's wrong? Are you hurt? I'll be right —"

"No. No, just listen. I know who killed her. It all fits, but there's no proof whatsoever. But I think you can get the proof."

"Who, Jane? Who are you talking about?"

"I'm afraid to say, for fear I'm wrong. But I know I'm not. No, what I'm most afraid of is that I'm *right*. Still — I'm sorry, I'm babbling. Give me a second." She covered the mouthpiece and took a long breath. "All right. Just listen. There are some things you have to do. Some information you have to get. If I'm right, that information will tell you all you need to know. First, call Evergreen Memories, that's a florist shop, and find out which of the suspects has been sent flowers recently. The paper was saved and wrapped around the flowers that were left on my porch.

"Next, tell the pathologist to test for aconite. If I'm right, that's what killed her.

"Third, you need to get some birth and death certificates from the State Department."

"Hold it, Jane. Birth and death certificates

233

are registered with individual states' vital statistics departments, not the State Department."

"Not if you're an American who's born or dies outside the country. I know, because that's where I have to get copies of mine."

"What name?"

"You'll have to ask Maria Espinoza that. Do you have a copy of Mrs. Pryce's autobiography?"

"Someplace. The teacher gave us one."

"Good. Find it. Look on page one twenty-eight. Question the maid about that page. Get names. Get the birth and death certificates from the State Department. Mel, my daughter's yelling for me. I think there's somebody at the door. I have to go —"

"But, Jane —"

She hung up.

"Mom, are you down there? Mrs. Nowack's here," Katie yelled down the steps.

"Be right up."

When she came back up the steps, Shelley and her mother were sitting at the kitchen table. "Jane, dear! What's wrong?" Cecily asked, getting up and putting her hand on Jane's forehead. "You're as white as a sheet."

"Where's Katie?" Jane asked quietly.

"Upstairs. Heading for the shower. What's wrong?"

"I'm going to tell you what I've done. I'm sure I'm right, but I hope desperately that I'm wrong. I know who killed Mrs. Pryce."

Shelley had paled slightly, but her voice was strong. "Do I guess from your expression that it's *not* Bob Neufield?"

"Oh, I feel like shit about this! Sorry, Mom."

"I've heard the word before, chickie. Sit down and tell us about it."

Jane opened Mrs. Pryce's book. "Read page one twenty-eight and think about the little birdcage. Oh, and don't anybody try to get in the guest bathroom. I've locked the flowers in there."

"I'm sure this is going to make some kind of sense," Shelley said, looking at Jane as if she'd snapped her last twig.

"The blue flowers are monkshood. Very poisonous."

"Poisonous!" Shelley yelped.

Cecily was reading the page Jane had directed her to. She looked up slowly and passed the book to Shelley. "Yes, yes. I think maybe I see what you mean. But who . . . ?"

— 20 —

Jane didn't expect to hear back from Mel during the morning. She knew he'd be too busy to call her. By noon, however, she was getting fretful. Her concerns about the murder, however, had to be put aside when, right on schedule at one o'clock, Thelma Jeffry's battleship gray Lincoln cruised into the drive. Jane hurried out to greet her youngest son — and of unfortunate necessity, her mother-in-law.

She took one look at Todd as he tumbled out of the car and gasped. "Todd! You must have gained ten pounds!"

He hugged her hard. "Yeah, Gramma let me eat anything I want. It was great, Mom-old-thing."

"Sure she did," Jane said through a forced smile. Thelma Jeffry, an angular, hard-edged woman, believed the way to any man's heart was to turn him into Porky Pig. "Thelma, you look like you've survived the ordeal," Jane said, coming around the car and helping her out.

"Oh, naturally. Children are quite

pleasant to travel with if you've got your own wits together," Thelma purred. The implication was clear: Jane had no wits to speak of and certainly never had them together. But Jane was glad to see that there were lines of fatigue around Thelma's eyes, and she looked awfully pale for a woman who'd just spent a week in Florida. "Cecily, how nice to see you," Thelma said.

Jane's mother had come out onto the porch. Todd ran and practically tackled her. Thelma watched this reunion with a cold eye.

Todd treated them to a solid hour of excited chatter about his trip, while Thelma sat stolidly listening. It was clear she was loathe to abandon him to his mother, much less his other grandmother, but was exhausted and longing to go home. She finally gave up the fight and left.

"Mom's leaving Monday. Do come to a big Sunday dinner, will you?" Jane asked Thelma as she tottered out to her car.

"That would be nice, dear. I do always enjoy hearing your mother talk about her . . . 'globe-trotting' life." She made it sound as if Cecily moved from campground to campground in a rusted-out pickup truck with a canvas tent in the back.

Todd met Jane as she went back in.

"Mom, do you think Nana would mind if I went over to Elliot's? I got a lot of stuff to show him."

"I'm sure Nana would understand. Ask her yourself, though."

A few minutes later, Jane and her mother were watching the driveway again. "Mike's due in about fifteen minutes. I'll be glad to have him back. Mom, I'm going to miss him horribly when he goes away to college. I depend on him so much."

"He's come through losing his father with flying colors, hasn't he?" Cecily said.

Jane nodded. "But it's not just the things he does. Mowing the lawn, carrying heavy things, fixing the dishwasher, all that male stuff. More important, he likes me. He and Todd both do. They think I'm a neat person who's worth talking to occasionally. But Katie —"

"It's just her age and hormones. One day she'll be a lovely young woman and she'll be your best friend. Like you're mine . . ."

Jane felt tears coming to her eyes. "Life *would* be awful without a mother," she said, just as a bright red Jeep turned in to the driveway. "There's Mike!"

This time she waited inside. Mike wouldn't appreciate his mother flying out the door and folding him in an embrace in front of his friend Scott.

He came in the door — tall, young, healthy, Jane's true pride and joy. Jane got teary again. She'd be holding up better, she knew, if it weren't for waiting for Mel to call and confirm her suspicions. She wasn't normally a weeper.

Mike had a packet of information from each college they'd visited. As he pulled out each one, Jane had to stop herself from crying, "Don't go so far away, please." She couldn't ever say that to him, least of all today when he was on the brink of going away and growing up entirely. He was so excited about leaving home.

When Todd came home, he took his grandmother upstairs to show her his hamsters (as if she hasn't been smelling the damned things for days, Jane thought). Jane got up to fix herself and Mike a soft drink while Mike stretched his long legs under the table. "Mom, I had a great time seeing those places."

"I'm glad, honey. How are you going to decide on which one to go to?"

"Well, I think maybe I've decided already."

"Oh? You've got a whole year to think about it."

"I think I'll just start out right here at

239

the junior college."

"Mike! Why? You aren't worried about the money, are you? I told you I can come up with —"

"No, Mom. It's not the money. It's you. I think you need me here."

Don't cry! Jane told herself. She set his drink down and took his big hands in hers. "Mikey, I do need you. But I don't want you to stay here because of me. I'll muddle along. Maybe when I'm eighty and getting around with a walker, I'll ask you to take care of me, but not until then."

"You sure?"

"Absolutely certain," she said with a lot more sincerity in her tone than she felt.

Uncle Jim Spelling called at four, barking as she picked up the phone, "Jane! I've just caught up on the papers. I didn't know about Mrs. Pryce. You stay out of this, you hear me!"

She considered explaining, but didn't have the heart or the energy. "I will, Uncle Jim. You're coming to dinner Sunday, aren't you?"

"Will the Dragon Lady be there?"

" 'Fraid so."

"Good. I haven't had a chance to rile her up for a long time. I'll be there. Jane, you do like I tell you. You and Cecily stay clear of that class business until the police sort this out. Are you listening to me? I mean it!"

By five-thirty, when she was starting dinner, Jane was a wreck. When the phone rang, she leaped for it, even though the last six calls had been Mike's friends welcoming him home.

"Jane?" Mel's voice.

"Yes?"

"I think you're right. I'm sorry."

Jane slid down the cabinet and sat on the floor. "Oh, so am I. When will you . . . ?"

"As soon as I'm sure."

"Mel, please don't tell anyone that I figured it out."

"I won't. I've got to go. I just wanted to tell you."

Mel hung up, but Jane couldn't move. Cecily found her still sitting on the floor. "Was that Mel? Were you right?"

"Yes. And I've never been sorrier about anything."

Missy, of course, knew nothing of what was going on behind the scenes and began the class with brisk enthusiasm. "I regret that I didn't schedule this as two-week course. You'll forgive me, I hope, if I race along and try to cover as much material as I can as quickly as possible. We're going to save the last hour of class tonight for critiquing the manuscripts I handed out to you before the class sessions started. Now, want to talk briefly about the value and use of photos, documents, and letters in an autobiography —"

For once, Jane didn't find herself automatically applying the information to her book — yes, it *was* becoming a book — about Priscilla. But she took notes assiduously, so that she wouldn't be tempted to look around at the class members. She was afraid of meeting the murderer's eyes. She knew if that happened, her own shame would flash like a neon light.

The first interminable hour passed and they took a short break, then reassembled. The tension was so thick that Jane wondered how anyone could breathe. But the others didn't seem to notice it. Or did they? Bob Neufield was staring at her, which made her skin crawl. When she met his gaze, his didn't falter. She looked away first. Grady was nervously tapping his pencil on the arms on his chair. Desiree was sitting at the back of the room, away from everyone else, and frowning at the blackboard as if there were something written there so faintly, she could hardly make it out. Naomi was struggling with the zipper on her purse as if closing it were of enormous importance, and Ruth was trying to help her, making little nervous, darting motions with her hands. Jane noticed that Cecily was humming under her breath, something she only did when she was very nervous, and even Shelley looked frightened.

Missy had just begun speaking again when the back door of the room opened. Jane didn't even notice at first, then she became aware of everyone craning to look back. She turned.

Mel was standing in the doorway.

Missy's lecture faltered to a stop. "Yes, can I help you, Detective VanDyne?"

"No. Please continue. I'm afraid I might have to ask you all to stay a little longer than usual."

"Why is that? What are you doing here?"

"I'm waiting for some information. When it arrives, you'll be free to leave," he said.

All but one of us, Jane thought.

He pulled a chair over by the doorway and sat down.

Jane glanced around the room. There was the illusion of guilt on every face. They were all perplexed and alarmed.

Missy continued, her voice trembling. "Very well. If you'll get out the manuscripts, I'd like to go over each one briefly.

243

First, I'll give my own comments and evaluations, then I'd like to know what impressions you had as you read them."

Everyone tried gamely to pretend that VanDyne wasn't at the back of the room, watching and listening. But their responses were feeble and disjointed.

The door opened again, bumping against VanDyne's chair. He moved it, and a uniformed woman officer handed him a white envelope. He thanked her, opened the envelope, and nodded. All illusion of a normal class was abandoned. Bob Neufield slammed his briefcase shut and glared at VanDyne. Grady got up and went to the front of the room to stand behind Missy's chair. Desiree Loftus leaned back and closed her eyes. Ruth and Naomi were holding hands. Cecily laid her hand on Jane's arm. Shelley was fidgeting with the lid of her pen, making a faint, frantic clicking sound.

Mel came into the middle of the room, in the aisle between the chairs. "I'm afraid I'm here to arrest the person whose name is on this birth certificate, the person who was born in captivity in the Philippines . . . Maxine Harbinger."

There was a moment of confused silence, quick, puzzled glances. Then Ruth Rogers stood up briskly, ruffles bouncing. "There's no need to make a fuss, Officer. I'm Maxine Ruth Harbinger."

"No, ma'am. You're not," VanDyne said softly.

Ruth stared at him.

"You can't save your sister," he went on very gently. "Not from the law — or from anything else."

Naomi Smith slowly got up and came to stand by her sister. She was normally a sickly, pale color. Now she was as white as death. "I'm sorry, Ruth. But you know I had to do it. I'd have happily killed her in the town square at high noon — with pride! — except I wanted to spare you. She killed our mother, Ruth. She had to be punished. You know that. It was necessary. It was right. Everything that happened to me after that was her fault. If we'd just had our mother —"

She was shaking, and near collapse. Ruth put her arm around her sister to support her and wept, "But the maid, Naomi. You almost killed the maid. You were too young to remember her, but she helped us in the prison camp after Mother died. She protected us from the guards and smuggled food in to us. She's the only reason *we* survived. And you almost killed her. That wasn't right."

Naomi was crying now, too. "But I didn't *mean* to, Ruth! Nobody else should have been hurt. It was only for that evil woman that killed our mother. You know I wouldn't harm anyone else for the world."

Ruth put both arms around her sister, in love and in physical support. Naomi was crumbling. Ruth looked over her shoulder and met Jane's eyes. "I know, Naomi. I know. Now, let's go with the police and explain it to them."

— 21 —

"Mom!" Katie called from the living room. "Mike and Todd are being repulsive again! They're such dweebs!"

"It's their nature," Jane called back from the dining room table.

"I'll help you clear this up," Thelma said, surveying the dirty dishes and general wreckage of Sunday dinner littering the table.

"No hurry, Thelma. More coffee, Uncle Jim? Mel? Mom?"

Shelley came into the room. "I've got my gang off to the pool. May I invite myself to dessert?" She sat down at Katie's abandoned place and helped herself to a microscopically thin wedge of strawberry pie. "Missy just called me. She said Naomi's in the hospital and is in very bad shape. Is that true, Mel?"

"Yes, it is. She won't make it to trial. It wasn't the arrest. We handled her with kid gloves. She just hasn't long to live." He glanced across the table at Jane.

"I'm not sure I understand yet, Jane,"

Thelma said grumpily. She'd expected the dinner conversation to center around her and her recent trip, but it hadn't. "Old Mrs. Pryce hadn't *actually* killed their mother, had she?"

"No, but she'd turned her in to the Japanese guards because she stole milk for her daughters," Jane said. "And the Japanese took care of the rest. Ruth and Naomi knew the story from other camp survivors, but they never knew the name of the woman, just that she was a general's wife. Then, when Missy handed out Mrs. Pryce's book and they saw the other side of the story, they recognized that this had to be the same person. Worse, in her book, Mrs. Pryce bragged about it, as if she'd done something noble and fine. It was too much for Naomi."

"Naomi Smith had a horrible life," Mel put in. "She was passed from one family to another, sexually abused in at least two of them. She felt that if her mother had lived, none of that would have happened to her. Which was probably true."

Thelma glared at him, offended that anyone would dare mention sex in any context at the table. "But why was the sister leaving clues for Jane? That makes no sense at all!"

"But it did, Thelma," Jane said. "She

knew Naomi had done it. She'd seen her reach toward Mrs. Pryce's plate and then palm a little bottle at the dinner table while everybody was looking for Grady's contact lens. When Mrs. Pryce died later that evening, Ruth was certain the bottle had contained poison. When she got home, she noticed that some of her monkshood had been picked, but there was no sign of the cut stalks anywhere. Naomi must have boiled it down — or whatever you do with it to make a concentrated poison. In their formative years in the prison camp, they both learned a lot about plants — which are edible and which are poison."

"Why didn't she just tell the police? I would have," Thelma said piously.

"It was her own sister, for God's sake!" Uncle Jim barked.

"Ruth not only loved her sister, she understood and probably sympathized with why she did it," Jane said. "And to be quite honest, I agree. But when Ruth learned that the maid had almost died, she couldn't stand it. She knew that Naomi had to be brought to justice for that horrible error. For all her surface fluffiness, Ruth's a very rigid person when it comes to morality. But she still couldn't bring herself to turn in her beloved sister."

"That doesn't answer my question. Why give all those incomprehensible clues to Jane?" Thelma asked. She didn't add, "of all people," but the implication hung in the air.

"Because she couldn't drop hints to the police," Jane explained. "The police don't have a house she could see from her house. If she'd sent them the birdcage, they wouldn't have known which crime it referred to, even if it came with a tag attached saying 'CLUE.' And I think the first one, the book, was meant for either Shelley or me. It was left in Shelley's car when Ruth knew where we were — at Bob Neufield's house because she sent me there with that library list. The cage could have gone to either of us, but the patio table appealed to her for some reason as a good place to leave it. Then, since I'd gotten that, I had to get the flowers."

"A book, a birdcage, and flowers," Jim Spelling mused. "I wouldn't have put that together and made anything of it."

"I didn't either at first," Jane admitted. "But you see, she was leading me along step by step. First the book that meant: 'The explanation is in here.' Then the bamboo cage, meaning: 'This is the part of the book.' The bamboo cage represented the

Japanese prison camp. Then the flowers, saying: 'This is how it was done.' "

"That's the part that makes me wild," Uncle Jim said. "She could have killed you with those damned flowers."

"No, not really," Jane said. "She knew I didn't have any children little enough to chew on flowers like a baby or toddler might. And none of us were likely to drink the water they were in. They don't exude a poisonous smell or anything. They scared me to death when I realized what they were, but they weren't really all that dangerous."

"I thought you said the flowers came from a florist," Thelma said. "It's downright irresponsible for a florist to send out —"

"No, they weren't from the florist, they were only wrapped in the florist's paper. Naomi had been hospitalized a few months ago and got lots of flowers. Ruth, being a frugal person, had automatically saved the paper — just because she saved everything that might come in handy someday. That was probably a legacy of the prison camp, too."

"The fact is, she didn't want to take the responsibility for ratting on her sister, so she dumped the moral dilemma in Jane's lap," Shelley said, cutting another paper-thin slice of pie. "What about the name, though?

How did Maxine Harbinger get to be Naomi Smith?" She glanced at VanDyne.

"Maxine *was* her first name. Like Ruth tried to claim it was hers, but some foster parent along the line didn't like it and called her by her middle name. Naomi. It stuck. She married briefly and got the Smith," he replied.

Thelma shook her head. "The woman set out to have her sister's crime revealed and then tried to claim that she herself was the murderer? I think she must have been insane."

"No," Shelley said. "She was very canny. I think she believed that Jane would keep quiet about the clues once she figured them out. That way, Ruth would have eased her own conscience by 'telling' someone, but Naomi wouldn't suffer the consequences. When it didn't turn out that way, she was horrified by what she'd done and wanted to protect Naomi. It wasn't such a bad plan, actually. Jane might well have felt so sorry for Naomi that she might have kept it to herself. And without her insight, the police would never have figured it out."

"Oh, I wouldn't be so sure of that," Mel said firmly. "We were on the track already."

"Mom!" Katie screeched from the family room. "Make them *stop!*"

Jane ignored her daughter and focused on Mel. "I beg your pardon? You had no idea! Admit it!"

"We did, too. We were checking out everything we could about everyone, including tracing to see whether Naomi's illness was real. One of the office staff was worrying away at the fact that a woman who lived in a middle-class suburb of Chicago had a blood disease that's only found in the tropics and in severely undernourished people. He'd discovered that she'd suffered from it all her life, and was already trying to find a birth certificate to see where she was born."

"Yes, and in another three years he might have figured it out if somebody had put a framed copy of the right page of Mrs. Pryce's book in front of him," Jane said indignantly.

Mel grinned at her. "Maybe sooner than that."

Thelma looked from Mel to Jane and back to Mel. She had a look of dawning suspicion.

Jim Spelling watched Thelma's eyebrows draw together, and he grinned at her wary expression.

Jane turned to Cecily. "It was all because they lost their mother. It's made me awfully glad I still have mine."

"Mom! They're terrible!" Katie screamed closer at hand.

Mike came tumbling into the room. He had Todd in a headlock. Todd was laughing hysterically and flailing his arms, trying to land a fist in his older brother's crotch.

Jane put her head in her hands. "Such a refined household," she moaned.

"No, that's not the way," Mel said, getting up and coming around the table. He pulled Todd away from Mike to demonstrate a better hold. "See, if you can get his shoulder this way, he can't use his arms —"

"Hold it," Uncle Jim said, coming to his feet. "That's all wrong. You've got it backwards. Here, let me show you." He grabbed Mel to demonstrate.

Thelma was making feeble little cries of alarm and disapproval.

Jane and Shelley looked at Cecily. "Don't they *ever* grow up?" Jane asked.

Cecily shook her head. "If your grandfather were here, he'd be right in the middle of it, knocking people around with his walker."

Jane got up. "Outside! All of you!" She started shoving them toward the door.

As they headed through the family room, Mel came back to Jane and whispered, "I've got some great holds I could show you later. How about it?" And with the gentlest of fanny pats, he was off to join the others in the backyard.

"Why, Jane," Thelma said when Jane came back to the dining room, "your face is red as a beet. You're not coming down with something, are you?"

Jane smiled.

The employees of Thorndike Press hope you have enjoyed this Large Print book. All our Thorndike and Wheeler Large Print titles are designed for easy reading, and all our books are made to last. Other Thorndike Press Large Print books are available at your library, through selected bookstores, or directly from us.

For information about titles, please call:

(800) 223-1244

or visit our Web site at:

www.gale.com/thorndike
www.gale.com/wheeler

To share your comments, please write:

Publisher
Thorndike Press
295 Kennedy Memorial Drive
Waterville, ME 04901